Ella J. Curtis

A Game of Chance

Vol. II

Ella J. Curtis

A Game of Chance
Vol. II

ISBN/EAN: 9783337067496

Printed in Europe, USA, Canada, Australia, Japan

Cover: Foto ©Andreas Hilbeck / pixelio.de

More available books at **www.hansebooks.com**

A NOVEL

BY

ELLA J. CURTIS

(SHIRLEY SMITH)

AUTHOR OF

"THE FAVOURITE OF FORTUNE," "ALL FOR HERSELF," "HIS LAST STAKE,"
ETC., ETC.

IN THREE VOLUMES

VOL. II

LONDON

HURST AND BLACKETT, LIMITED

13, GREAT MARLBOROUGH STREET

1889

PRINTED BY
TILLOTSON AND SON, MAWDSLEY STREET
BOLTON

CONTENTS

OF

THE SECOND VOLUME.

CONTENTS OF THE SECOND VOLUME.

A GAME OF CHANCE.

CHAPTER I.

HUSBAND AND WIFE.

WHEN the excitement of the wedding was over, the evening promised to be unusually quiet in Halkin Street. Sir John and Miss Lambton dined quietly together at half-past seven, and the meal was about half over, when a sharp ring at the hall door bell announced a late and unexpected visitor. Someone came in, and Miss Lambton, whose ears were very sharp, turned first red and then pale, and said, in great agitation—

"It is very like Letty's voice, John. What can be the matter?"

Sir John burst out laughing. " Letty, indeed," he said.

The butler was at his elbow as he spoke, "Miss Erskine — Mrs. Herbert Otway — I beg pardon, Sir John," he said, "is in the library and wishes to see you."

Sir John rose in a hurry and threw his dinner napkin among the dishes. " Bless my soul!" he cried, "what has happened now?"

And in the library, sure enough, he found his daughter; not calm, cold and contemptuous, but in a state of the most violent agitation. "Oh papa — papa!" she cried, clinging to him, "I thought I should never get here. I have come back to you, papa. I cannot stay with him! It is of no use to ask me; it would kill me! Do not ask any questions, please, but keep me with you always! Do not let me be taken away!"

" But you must be mad, child ; completely
out of your senses ! You marry a man of
your own free will at twelve and run away
from him before eight.   No one ever heard
of such a thing.   What in the world came
between you ?   You went away like a pair of
turtle-doves !"

"Oh, I don't know, I don't know ! It is
only that I dislike him so much."   The girl
sobbed as she suddenly broke down, and just
then little Miss Lambton stole into the room,
and stood inside the door wringing her hands.
"Oh, my poor child !   My poor, dear child !"
was all she could say.

Sir John began to get angry.   " I insist
upon knowing what it means," he said,
sternly.

" It has no meaning, except that I dislike
him too much to live with him," Letty sobbed
out.

" But are you aware, you foolish girl, that,
as your husband, he can make you ?"

In the middle of her sobs Letty laughed. "He make me! He will beg and pray," she said, "but that is all he will do."

"But the law gives him rights," Sir John persisted. "You are as much his property as his tables and chairs. I dare not keep you when he comes here and insists upon having you."

"Indeed," she said; "is that so? Then if he insists, I suppose I must go; but you will keep me for to-night, will you not, papa?"

"Well, for to-night, of course, you must stay here. Oh, Louise, are you there? Just see who that is knocking at the door, will you?"

It was the butler with a telegram.

"This is from Otway," cried Sir John.

It was very concise. "Reply at once and say if your daughter is with you."

"And now I wonder what will happen next," said Sir John, as he took a form and wrote his reply. It contained but three words, " She is here."

Two days passed and the deserted bridegroom made no sign. The runaway bride shut herself up in her own room, and saw no one but her aunt, who was a most consoling companion, for she praised and blamed exactly as she was expected to do. With her father, Letty was in deep disgrace; but at the end of the second day he relented a little, chiefly because he was hurt and offended with Otway for having taken no steps to bring about a reconciliation.

The third morning, however, brought a curt, but very polite note, to the effect that Mr. Otway would be glad to see Sir John Erskine on business. Letty was not even mentioned.

" He will probably want to see me, papa," the young lady said, indifferently, "and I suppose I cannot refuse. It will be very disagreeable, but of course, this kind of thing cannot go on. You say that, having married him, I must put up with him; so if he asks to see me, you can send him up to the drawing-room."

The interview between Sir John and his son-in-law was short and rather stormy. The view taken by Otway of Letty's conduct was so unexpected that it left her father absolutely without a word to say in her defence; and at last, glad of an excuse to let the two most interested in the issue of the affair come together and patch up a truce, if truce were possible, he told Otway that Letty was prepared for his visit and sent him upstairs.

No greeting, even of the most formal kind, passed between them when he went into the room. Letty's face was flushed, and she was trembling with excitement; Otway was apparently calm, but when he saw her his self-control was sorely tried.

"Your father told me you were here," he said. He leaned with one hand on the table, as he stood facing her; she was seated at a little distance; the light fell upon her, and never had she looked prettier or more captivating in his eyes.

"I came—what do you suppose I came for?" he said. She expected a torrent of reproaches, and he asked a question in a cold, measured voice.

The change in his manner was too marked not to strike her, and she faltered out "I—I do not know."

"You may perhaps imagine, judging me by the past," he went on with a little laugh, "that I came to beg—to implore of you to come back to me; perhaps you think I came to kneel at your feet, to entreat for your love; to beseech of you in your goodness to come to my arms and accept me as your husband. But do not be afraid; the law gives me rights over you, as perhaps you know. I could compel you to live under my roof as my wife, but I am not going either to beg or to enforce. Having left me as you did, you evidently wish to live apart from me; besides, you told me in the plainest possible language that you did not care for me — that you shrank from my touch and loathed my caresses. If a man does not understand such words he is a fool; and, being a fool, I did not understand at first, but I do now, and we will live apart. I make no appeal to your pity or your forbearance—love not existing, I cannot appeal to it—but Letty, remember that you have outraged and insulted as pure and true a love as ever man felt for woman. No husband could love with more passion and devotion than I loved you— you cruel, heartless girl—when I put that ring on your finger a few days ago. A few days! It seems months, years almost, since I stood with your hand in mine and believed you were mine for evermore. But now I am awake as if from a long sleep, in which love for you debased my manhood, and made me

a puppet and plaything in your thoughtless
hands. Yes, I am awake now, ; my strength
has come back to me. I have not quite
conquered my love, for a passion like mine
does not die in an hour, but I can leave you,
for I despise you. I do not insult you by
reminding you that my honour is in your
hands, for it is your honour also ; we are
man and wife, and unless you wish to have
the bond legally set aside, man and wife we
must remain. I shall take no step in the
matter, but neither shall I make any objection
if you wish to be free."

To say that Letty was amazed and con-
founded at this unexpected address from the
man who had hitherto been swayed, like a
reed in the wind, by a glance from her eyes,
is to give a very inadequate idea of her
feelings at the moment. So bewildered was
she, that she would have liked to make him
repeat it all over again, that she might try to
understand his meaning clearly. Was it

really Herbert Otway who was standing
there before her, with those stern, unloving
eyes? Was that his voice that addressed
her in those cold, measured tones, and
that uttered such contemptuous and cutting
words?

She tried in vain to answer him, but not a
word would come; she sat with her eyes on
the ground and a deep flush of shame and
intense mortification burned on her face.
And with these visible signs of perturbation,
there was a wild storm of pride battling in
her heart with another strange and per-
plexing emotion, the very existence of which
she had not suspected until that moment.

"I am glad to see you have the grace to
blush," he went on, mercilessly. "I have
blushed for you many times since that evening
at Richmond, when you left me to be the
laughing-stock of the men and women who
helped me to search the empty house for
you. But since that night I have blushed

more for my own folly in having loved you.
You will be glad to know, I am sure, that the
cure of my madness has begun ; indeed, you
showed me yourself how to begin, and for
that I thank you. But it might be a blow to
your vanity were I to tell you how I begin
to rejoice in my freedom."

After that she could bear no more. Anger
and mortification—and with them was still
that other feeling, as yet unnamed, which
prompted her to fling herself at his feet to
implore his forgiveness—got the better of
her ; she rose and faced him boldly. " You
have said enough—more than enough," she
cried, hotly, "and I must beg to be left alone.
Everything you say only proves that our
marriage would be a most unhappy one, and
that it is better to part in time, and that—
that—but I cannot answer you properly—
you have been very—rude." Words failed
her ignominiously, and she knew that tears
were coming to complete her mortification.

And had those tears but welled over, the victory would have been with her! As it was, at the sight of her beautiful face, with that unknown look of alarm and distress upon it, his sternness was fast melting away. "But suppose," whispered pride, "you meet with another rebuff; remember she does not love you." And how glad he was that he had resisted the passing weakness when, raising her head with an imperious gesture, Letty said—

"I am sorry to be obliged to ask you, for the second time, to leave me, Mr. Otway."

"I obey your command with infinite pleasure," he answered, with dignity equal to her own; and backing to the door, apparently in order to make an effective exit, but in reality to see, until the very last moment, the face that was so lovely, and, for all his boasting, still so dear, he bowed low and disappeared.

Letty remained standing where he left her until the sound of his footsteps died away upon the stairs ; then she threw up her arms with a despairing gesture, and broke out into passionate weeping.

And if the sound of those tempestuous tears had but reached the man whose bitter taunts had called them forth, he would have learned that, just as he repaid her with scorn for scorn, his wife's heart was won.

CHAPTER II.

MISTRESS AND MAID.

A YEAR and some months subsequent to the marriage and immediate separation of Mr, and Mrs. Herbert Otway, Mr. or, as he now was, Captain and Mrs. John Erskine were at Simla. Young John, as he was still called, not at the Chase but at Little Centre Bridge, had been appointed, soon after the birth of his son, *aide-de-camp* to his Excellency the Governor-General, and this post of honour was a source of infinite satisfaction to Mrs. Erskine; for in the first place, it took her away from the "regiment," and for one cause or another, known only to the women themselves, she, and the wives of her husband's brother officers, did not get on too well together.

It is quite possible that Mrs. Erskine was too popular with men to be liked by women ; it is also a fact that she gave herself "airs" —traded on her popularity in fact, and made enemies right and left. A fruitful source of gossip and scandal at once dried up at its spring when the Erskines went to Calcutta ; but stray rumours of Mrs. Erskine's triumphs at Government House were wafted from time to time to the distant station she had left with such satisfaction, and when it was known that she was enjoying the delights of the favourite Hill Station, while many of those she had so often eclipsed by her beauty were obliged to swelter in the plains, envy was the dominant passion in every female breast, and much loud - spoken pity was lavished upon that "poor deluded Captain Erskine."

But if John Erskine had any real cause for

unhappiness, he contrived to hide it from the
world very successfully.   It would not be
absolutely true to say that marriage with
the woman of his choice had dispelled no
illusions, or even substituted, for the heartaches of love, heartaches now and then of
a different kind ; but, on the whole, he and
Amy got on very well.   Unlike her unknown
sister-in-law, Letty, who had quarrelled with
her husband on her wedding-day, for seemingly no better reason than his excessive
fondness for her, Mrs. Erskine could not,
she affirmed, have lived with a man who did
not give way to her in everything, and whose
eyes were not so blinded by love that he could
see no faults.   She held the whip and reins,
and woe betide her steed if he shied, or
showed the slightest desire to kick over
the traces, or get the bit between his teeth.
John Erskine was patient and docile to a
fault ; and if he erred in over-indulgence to
his beautiful wife, he had the satisfaction of

being envied the possession of such a lovely woman wherever and whenever she appeared.

As soon as she arrived in Calcutta, and was seen in what might be called the train of the Governor-General, she laid herself out for conquests more brilliant than any she had yet achieved, and having learned by experience how foolish she was to make enemies of women, she struck out a new line, and did her best to captivate her own sex also. She succeeded fairly enough, but whether her heart was not really in the work, or whether it is true that women never take very kindly to women, she was still the favourite of the men, and among the men she had, of course, her special favourites, although no one man could boast with truth that he had been singled out from among his fellows.

There was one who hoped that he was first in favour, but Mrs. Erskine encouraged his visits for the simple reason that he brought her plenty of news and gossip, and she was unkind enough to laugh at him behind his back. It was very ungrateful of her so to do, for he was always ready to fetch and carry for her, and at a ball she could always say she was engaged to " Gus Lewin," if an objectionable partner presented himself.

Being also one of his Excellency's *aides*, this good-looking, but not specially fascinating or dangerous young man, migrated to Simla with the rest of the Viceregal Court, and he was a constant visitor at the pretty bungalow inhabited by the Erskines. Mrs. Erskine could have lived in one of those provided for the Government officials, but she insisted upon a much larger and more comfortable residence, that stood among the rhododendron groves and pines which cover the mountain with the double summit on which Simla is built.

This roomy bungalow was perhaps some-

what lonely, being, in a measure, isolated
and shut in ; but Mrs. Erskine was perfectly
satisfied with it.   Those visitors who were
anxious to enjoy her society thought nothing
of the ride from the town, indeed a longer
pilgrimage could be borne when it was
remembered that, at the end, was that
delicious verandah, cool and shady, with
chairs standing about to tempt men who
were lazy to lounge, or to teach energetic
men, if there are any in Simla, how to be
lazy.   And the beautiful mistress, who either
reclined in a hammock or upon a heap of
cushions, was very charming to look upon, if
she was not strikingly brilliant or original in
conversation.

She was more often to be found upon her
cushions than in her hammock, for she had
not quite mastered the difficulties of getting
in and out of it gracefully ; this was a great
disappointment to her, as she had lately read
a well-known Indian romance, the scene of

which is laid in Simla, and she thought it
would be very "fetching" if she could imitate
the charming heroine of the book by appear-
ing in a hammock.

But on a beautiful afternoon, about a month
after the migration to Simla, the verandah
was deserted, and Mrs. Erskine was under
the hands of her maid. She had been for a
ride, and she was about to change her dress
for luncheon ; some men were coming out
with her husband, for a polo match was to
take place between four and five.

"You have not put out a dress for me,
Rossitur,"—she was always called by her
maiden name—the lady said, when the maid
appeared in answer to her mistress's bell.

"I understood you were going to the polo
match, madam," was the answer, "and that
you would lunch in your habit."

"I have changed my mind ; I am not
going. It is too hot."

Rossitur's lips parted in a peculiar smile, as

she turned away to take out a dress to re-
place the habit.

"You can go if you like," Mrs. Erskine
continued, as the maid began to brush out
and arrange her hair. "Pottinger can take
you. By-the-bye, how is he to-day?"

"He complained a good deal of his head
last night; but he seems quite well again to-
day."

"I saw little Georgy this morning," Mrs.
Erskine went on. "Your master says he
wishes his boy looked as strong as yours,
Rossitur."

"But mine is a month older, madam."

"Oh, that is nothing. Jack is a very tiny
mite for his age; but I am sure I cannot help
it."

"No, madam; you nursed him as long as
you could."

"And are you sure you do not care to go
to the polo match, Rossitur?"

"Quite sure, madam. The mail goes

out to-morrow, and I want to write to my sister."

"And I have never written to John's people at the Chase. Not one line have they had from me since I was married. But I cannot write to people I never saw, can I, Rossitur?"

"It must be rather difficult, madam. Have master's sister and her husband made up their quarrel? You told me, madam, you remember, that they separated on their wedding-day."

"No; she is still living at home, and I do not think they ever meet. How is that brother of yours getting on—the musician? Oh! you have but one, have you? Well; how is he?"

"Very well, I believe, madam. He never writes to me himself, but Alice, my sister, tells me about him."

"And she told you, I remember, about his giving lessons on the organ to Lady Judith someone. What has become of her?"

" She was at home the whole of last autumn and winter, and Alice said in her last letter there was a report in the village that she was engaged to a very rich man."

" And you were in hopes that she would marry your brother, weren't you ?"

An angry flush rose to Rossitur's face.

" If she liked him well enough to run after him," she said, " she ought to marry him. Alice says he thinks of nothing but her. He may not have a title, but he's good enough for any lady in England."

Mrs. Erskine laughed.

" You used to think yourself good enough for any gentleman in India, Rossitur ; and yet you married George Pottinger."

" And I was a fool for my pains!" Rossitur broke out angrily—she was evidently not much in awe of her mistress. " I put a log round my neck I can never get rid of the day I went to church with him."

" Oh, you say so now," said Mrs. Erskine ;

"but I always thought, and I still think, you were a very lucky girl; and when Captain Erskine settles at the Chase some day—and no one can tell what may happen; Sir John might break his neck out hunting any day next winter—you and Pottinger shall have one of the lodges; or you might set up an inn in the town."

"Thank you, madam," said Rossitur, and this time she stooped to pick up a hairpin in order to hide her smile.

"Now I am ready," Mrs. Erskine said, "and you may take my crewel work and those books out to the verandah and see if your master has come."

In five minutes Rossitur came back and announced that Captain Erskine and three gentlemen were waiting for her to go in to lunch.

"Who are they, Rossitur?"

Rossitur named the three, one after the other, and Mrs. Erskine, having taken a

last survey of herself in the mirror, left the
room to join her husband.

"She is expecting someone who has not
come," Rossitur said to herself, as she set
about to arrange the room and put away
the various articles that were scattered about.
"And she says I may go and see the polo.
That looks as if she wanted to get me out of
the way ; and yet why should she, for there
is no more harm in having Mr. Lewin here
to-day to gossip to her on the verandah than '
there was in his being here yesterday ? But
then he was not the only one yesterday !
And Pottinger and I can have one of the
lodges, or set up an inn in the town ! Much
obliged, Mrs. Erskine, I'm sure. Only for
you and your husband I might have married
a gentleman, and had a maid for myself.
Yes, and I'll have one yet ! I am as handsome as ever you were, my lady, and I know
I have more brains. Who is there ? Oh,
it's you, is it ?" as our old acquaintance, Pot-

tinger appeared. "What business have you here ?"

"I only came to tell you," he said, "that luncheon is over, and there's a fine row going on between my master and your mistress."

"Oh, you always have some story!" cried Rossitur, derisively. "And half your time you don't know what you're saying!"

"Don't I ? I know you're a——"

"That will do!" she interrupted, holding up her finger. "You will call me a liar once too often perhaps. What are they quarrelling about ?"

"Because she will not go and see him play polo."

"The best thing he can do is to stay at home and help her to entertain her visitor."

"Does she expect anyone ?"

"She did not tell me ; but perhaps if one comes I might send a message to the Captain."

"There will be murder if you do," said

Pottinger. He was standing in the half-open door as he spoke.

His wife laughed.

" Bella," he said, "do you ever think of the night poor Jem Hathaway shot himself in the Stillingfort Woods? Don't you try to make master jealous of his wife."

Rossitur's dark eyes flashed angrily upon him ; but, before she could speak he heard Captain Erskine's voice calling to him, and away he ran.

CHAPTER III.

JACK ERSKINE'S WIFE.

WHEN Pottinger told his wife that his master and her mistress were quarrelling, he had slightly exaggerated facts, even as he knew them, for, in the vulgar sense of the term, they never quarrelled. There were not infrequent scenes, and occasionally they ended in a fit of the sulks on the part of the wife, and in penitence and a costly present to "make peace" with, on the part of the husband.

This particular afternoon Captain Erskine was surprised and disappointed when Amy appeared at luncheon not in riding dress; but then it was quite possible for her to put on her habit again before it was time to start for the polo ground, so he said nothing.   But, in answer to a question from one of her guests, she said she was not going to the match, and when pressed for a reason by another, she answered, without giving a thought to what she said, that her little boy was not very well.

Erskine, who was devoted to his child, took alarm at once.

"What is the matter with the kid?" he said.   "He was all right this morning."

Amy looked at him as much as to say, "What a dear old stupid you are not to see that I am making an excuse," and answered, in her sweetest manner, "Oh, it is nothing of any consequence; he seemed a little languid, that is all."

"Languid! But he oughtn't to be languid. Have you sent for anyone?   I can't go and play polo if the boy is not well."

"My dear John," said Mrs. Erskine, sharply, "the boy is perfectly well. Do not make such a ridiculous fuss about nothing."

"Then why did you say he wasn't?" Erskine muttered; and after that he left the burden of conversation upon his wife and the guests. He knew by experience Amy's little habit of making false excuses serve the place of true ones, and to be obliged to suspect her of not being absolutely truthful always made him angry.

He took his friends away after luncheon to smoke on the verandah, and then, making some excuse, he went back to the dining-room to his wife.

"What is this about the boy, Amy?" he said. "Is he ill or well?"

"Perfectly well," she answered, readily. "Could you not see that I had to say something to put that man off."

"I wish you had not said *that*," he retorted. "I might have known it was only an excuse. But why can't you come if Jack is all right?

I thought you were looking forward to the match."

"Not I, indeed! I am sick of polo. I never intended to go, although I said nothing about it."

"You never intended! Come now; that is a stretch of imagination. Why, all last week you talked of nothing else!"

"But, all the same, I never intended to go," she repeated. "You must allow me to know what I meant to do better than you."

"And what are you going to do all the afternoon?" he inquired. "I suppose you expect a lot of fellows from town?"

"I expect no one. I am going to write letters—probably. Do you remember that to-morrow is mail day?"

"The day after, as it happens."

"Rossitur told me to-morrow. But no matter; it is as well to be in time."

"I wish you would write to some of my people at the Chase. You are always

promising to do it, and you never do it.   I
know they think it very odd that you never
send them a line."

" Well, perhaps I may be able to manage
it this mail—if I have time.   But I have to
write to my sister in Florida.   By the way,
she said in her last letter that her brother-in-
law, Herbert Otway, had just left them and
gone back to England.   Is there any chance
of a reconciliation between him and your
sister ?   It must be very awkward for a girl
to be married and yet not married, as she
is."

"Yes; it is a rum business altogether ; but
you know when Filmer wrote to me he said
she didn't care a straw for Otway.   I wish
she hadn't married him.   And so you are
going to write this afternoon ?   You will
please yourself, I suppose, but I think you
might come and see me play."

" But you are not such a wonderful player,
you know."

" I know nothing about it. I am as good as your friend Lewin any day."

"My friend Lewin, as you call him, is one of the best players in India."

Erskine burst out laughing.

"So he says himself. He's not a bad hand at boasting, everyone knows."

" I would not sneer at him, Jack, if I were you ; people might imagine you were jealous. By the way, which side does he play on this afternoon ?"

" You know perfectly well he doesn't play at all. Hasn't he had his arm in a sling for a week past ?"

" Oh ; so he has. I forgot."

" And it was only yesterday you were tying it up shorter for him ! You thought I didn't see the performance, I suppose. Beast ! I wish he was dead !"

" Dear me ; how ferocious we are to-day ! But you need not be jealous of poor Gus Lewin. When he comes to see me he either reads poetry or recites it. It is all the same to me, for I always go to sleep. I assure you he is not an atom more interesting than you are yourself. If it were Victor de——Good gracious, Jack, what is the matter? Why mayn't I speak of poor Victor?"

"Because I hate him."

"And I do not. What a rage you always get into if I only mention his name! Surely you ought to be satisfied when you know I refused him and married you."

"He had better not show his face here."

"How can he show his face when he is hundreds of miles away? I am sure I don't want to see the poor fellow, if his coming is to rub you up the wrong way. I wish you would contrive to keep your temper. Sometimes I think you are as mad as Pottinger. Rossitur tells me he was very bad last night."

"Any man would be bad with such a——"

"Hush! She is nothing of the kind; but

if that man breaks out some day and murders us all in our beds, perhaps you will be convinced."

"If he would begin with Rossitur I shouldn't mind. I hate that woman more and more every day."

"She is probably at work in the next room and listening to your compliments."

"I do not care if she was in this room ; and I'll be bound she's listening wherever she is. I hate her, and I believe she will do us some harm before she stops."

"What can she do ? Really, Jack, you get more silly every day ! Isn't it time you were going to your polo ?"

"I have a great mind not to go at all."

"Then stay by all means ; but, if you stay, I go ; so please make up your mind quickly."

"Oh! I am going ; do not be afraid. I should not like to interfere with your little arrangements."

And he went to the door.

"Good-bye," she said, pleasantly. "Come back in a better temper."

"Perhaps I shall not come back at all. Men have been killed playing polo before to-day !"

"Oh, yes, you will!" she answered, smiling at him. "Naught was never in danger, you know. There now. Don't frown like that. Can you not take a joke ?"

"Yes ; when it's meant!" he muttered.

Then he opened the door and called "Pottinger! Pottinger!" and, leaving his wife, Pottinger ran to his master.

An hour later, when it might be presumed that the polo match was in full swing—for the ground was not more than a quarter-of-an-hour's ride from the bungalow — Mrs. Erskine was seated on a low chair in the verandah ; there was a piece of fancy work on her lap, and some books were scattered about within reach of her hand ; but her eyes were closed, and she looked the picture of indolence.

Beside her was a man a year or two older than her husband ; not bad looking, but somewhat heavy in feature, and by no means animated in expression. He was stretched out at his ease in a lounging chair, his left arm rested in a sling, and there was an open book turned face downwards on his knee. It was Captain Lewin's highest ambition to pose as a literary character ; his pretentions were based upon a solitary contribution to *Punch*, sent in when he was a lad of eighteen, and inserted, much to his surprise ! His friends declared that he had never written anything but an advertisement to the "Agony Column" of the *Times*, but that was not true. He was the proud author of an epigram in *Punch*.

Just to amuse herself, Mrs. Erskine had pretended to foster his ambition, and the result was, that when they were alone, he, instead of carrying on a flirtation, as was suspected by Captain Erskine, used to read aloud if the lady were inclined to listen. But she was not always in the mood ; so, unless she happened to be either pre-occupied or too lazy to talk, he did not venture to do more than produce a volume, and on more than one occasion he had been known to read her to sleep.

She was not in a talking mood this afternoon, so the book was brought out and the reading began ; but it had not gone on very long when she felt herself getting drowsy, and if she had not roused herself by a great effort she would have been fast asleep.

" It would be so much nicer if you would talk, Gus," she said. All his lady friends called Captain Lewin "Gus." " I have not heard one word of that book for the last ten minutes. Surely there must be some news. Is anyone going to run away with anyone ? I thought it was the correct thing for people

to elope when they came to the Hills;
Captain Erskine never tells me any scandal,
so I have to look to my friends."

"Nothing interesting has happened as yet;
everyone says it will be an exceptionally
proper dull season.   There is only one
grass-widow in the place, and she is forty-
five and very ugly."

"Oh, dear! what *are* we to do to get up a
little excitement?   Are there no new people
for one to go and see?"

"There are no new women, but there is a
new man!   An old friend of yours, too, someone said.   That handsome Frenchman who
used to be in Calcutta—what is his name?—
do you remember?"

He was not looking at his companion or
he must have noticed the strange pallor that
suddenly overspread her face; she caught up
her fan, and began to use it vigorously.

"I remember him," she said, presently,
and in her own ears her voice had a strange

note in it. "Captain Erskine and I were talking of him after luncheon to-day. Does he make any stay in Simla?"

"Oh; I don't know the man at all, so I can't tell you; but you are sure to see him."

Mrs. Erskine made no reply; her eyes were fixed upon the short road that led from the house to the entrance gate. A man, who had just dismounted and given up his horse to a groom, was approaching slowly, and, a moment or two after he came in sight, she rose hurriedly, and remained standing until he reached the verandah.

He was young, of slender, graceful build; and when he took off his hat he showed a closely-cropped head of dark hair; pale, olive complexion, and singularly beautiful soft, dark eyes. There was in them now an indescribable expression as he came forward and took Mrs. Erskine's outstretched hand.

" I heard just this moment that you were in Simla," she said. " Captain Lewin, allow me to introduce Monsieur Victor de Louvain."

CHAPTER IV.

THE FATAL MESSAGE.

IT might have been half-an-hour after the arrival of the second visitor, that Rossitur, coming suddenly into the drawing-room—it opened into that part of the verandah always occupied by Mrs. Erskine—found Captain Lewin fast asleep on a couch. She was so surprised to see him that she started violently and made a faint exclamation. It was quickly checked, however, for Rossitur never betrayed herself unnecessarily; and her object in entering the room at that moment was simply to spy upon her mistress, and to hear, if possible, what she and her visitor had to say to one another. Hence

her astonishment when she found him asleep
on the sofa.

"He never did that before when he was
here alone," the maid said, as she stole softly
to the open window and looked out.

Mrs. Erskine, not half-asleep now, was
leaning back in her favourite chair, and on a
heap of cushions beside her sat the second
visitor, who was immediately recognised by
Rossitur.   The pair were engaged in earnest
conversation, but the man was the principal
speaker.   Amy Erskine was looking bril-
liantly handsome; her cheeks were slightly
flushed, and the long lashes that rested on
her cheeks — her eyes were cast down —
seemed darker even than usual in contrast to
the soft masses of her flaxen hair.

Her companion's eager talk was nothing
but a short history of his life since he and
Mrs. Erskine had parted before her marriage;
there was not a word spoken by him to
intimate that she had been more to him than

a pleasant acquaintance ; but, in the hearts
of both at the moment there were sleeping
memories of by-gone happy days, and to stir
them into life would have been an unwise
enterprise for either. But there was no
danger. Victor de Louvain was, in every
sense of the word, a man of honour.

But Bella Rossitur was a woman to whom
the word had no meaning ; she knew, no one
better, how strong had been the attachment
between the two who were now talking
together so quietly, and, being base herself,
she was ready to attribute baseness to others.
Here was an opportunity to make mischief,
or, failing that, to make her master unhappy.
There was no love lost between Rossitur and
Captain Erskine, and it would give her infinite satisfaction to do him some real injury ;
or, failing that, to make him suspicious and
miserable in his domestic relations. He was
but too well inclined to be jealous of his
beautiful wife, and he could not be ignorant

of the fact that an engagement of some kind had at one time existed between her and Monsieur de Louvain.

But how was the seed to be sown that was to bear bitter fruit? If she could in any way convey a message to Captain Erskine to the effect that the Frenchman had arrived at the bungalow in his absence, the thing would be done. And to send a written message to the polo ground would be the easiest thing in the world. There were always three or four idle grooms about, and she could scribble a few lines and send them off forthwith ; there was not the slightest fear that her master would betray her to his wife, and her mistress would never suspect her.

As she was moving rapidly away from the window the skirt of her dress overturned a light chair, and, at the noise made by its fall, Mrs. Erskine started and looked round.

" Is that you, Rossitur ?" she said.

" Yes, madam," the maid replied at once.

" I came in to see if you wanted anything ; I did not know you were engaged."

Begging her companion to excuse her for a moment, Mrs. Erskine went into the room, and, drawing Rossitur away towards the door, she asked in a low, eager voice if she had seen the gentleman on the verandah.

Rossitur answered briefly in the affirmative.

" Then I want you, if you please," Mrs. Erskine continued, " not to mention to Captain Erskine that he was here to-day ; he is in Simla for a very short visit, and I do not want your master to know that he came to see me. You understand ?"

" Perfectly," Rossitur answered.

" Of course, there is no harm in his coming to see me; but Captain Erskine is so peculiar, and dislikes French people so much, that it is as well not to vex him for nothing. I know I can depend upon you, Rossitur."

" You can, madam."

" Monsieur de Louvain asked if you were

still with me, and wanted to know if you were as handsome as ever. You might bring us some coffee presently, and then he can see for himself."

"And shall I wake Captain Lewin, madam?" Rossitur asked, with a glance at the sofa."

"Oh, yes; wake him of course; but it doesn't matter; he is sure to wake up presently."

But before Rossitur brought the coffee and was complimented by de Louvain on her appearance, she despatched a tiny note to the polo ground, with directions that it was to be delivered into Captain Erskine's own hands. It contained these words—

"If you come back at once, you will find that your wife remained at home this afternoon to receive Monsieur Victor de Louvain."

The third and concluding game of the polo match was about to begin when Rossitur's messenger rode up and presented his master with the note. Erskine, thinking it was of no moment—a message from Amy perhaps to tell him to bring someone back to dinner— held it unopened, while he eagerly discussed the games that had already been lost and won. He had mounted a fresh pony, and it was already wild with excitement to be off; but, reining it in tightly, he finished what he had to say about the play, and then opened the note and read its brief contents.

Those who were grouped about him remembered afterwards that he turned deadly white, a sure sign with him of anger and excitement; then he replaced the note in the envelope, crumpled both up in his hand, and jumped to the ground, calling out, " Someone must take my place. I can't play ; I am wanted at home."

A dozen voices cried out that he must finish the match.

" Is anyone ill, old fellow ?" one man said.

" Is it the kid or Mrs. Erskine ?" cried another.

" No ; there is no one ill—nothing the matter," he answered ; " but I want to be off—there is someone I want to see." Then, after hesitating a moment, he sprang upon his pony again, calling out, " I'm ready ! Come on, all of you !" and muttering to himself, " An hour hence will do as well for him," he threw himself headlong into the game.

But more than one of those present suspected that something had happened to put him out ; always a bold and dashing player, he was now reckless in the extreme. He was now here and now there—the ball seemed to fly under his dashing strokes, and an ignorant spectator might have been pardoned if he had thought that a fight was going forward instead of a game.

At last, when the pursuit was hottest, there was a sudden cry indicative of dismay and alarm! In a moment every player had flung aside his club, and they were seen hastening, one and all, towards a spot in the centre of the ground. A pony was galloping wildly about the field, but its rider, young John Erskine, would never mount it again! When his comrades in the game came up he was already dead. A sudden stumble of the pony — it was going at full speed — had pitched him clean over its head; his neck was broken and he died instantaneously.

Several of his friends were on their knees beside him, and one was trying to pour some brandy through his clenched teeth, when an excited figure broke through the group, and Pottinger, Erskine's faithful soldier servant, flung himself beside the body. He seemed almost beside himself with grief, as, forcing open the mouth with a wrench the others had not dared to use, he seized the flask and poured the contents down the throat that would never taste food or drink again.

Then they all watched for some sign of life ; but the handsome young face seemed to grow more white and rigid as they gazed ; and at last, one of those nearest put out his hand and gently closed the fast glazing eyes.

" Poor Jack !" he said. " He played like a madman ! I am afraid he had some bad news in that note someone brought him."

" Here it is in his glove," said another, drawing it out.

The note was doubled together in its envelope, and, having flattened it out, the man who found it handed it over to Pottinger.

" Is that Mrs. Erskine's writing ?" he asked.

Pottinger hesitated a moment, and then answered, shortly,

" Yes."

" Then she has the best right to it," said the other. " Its contents are sacred to us. Take it, my man, and give it to her as it is."

Pottinger touched his cap, and slipped

the note into his pocket. But, although his action was quiet now, and his manner respectful, they all noticed that his excitement was only subdued, not conquered, as he stood by and listened while they consulted together as to the best means of breaking the awful news to the widow. There was not a man among them who did not shrink from the office, and when Pottinger said at last, " She knows me best, gentlemen ; let me do it," they sent him.

Mrs. Erskine was seated at the piano, playing while Victor de Louvain sang. Captain Lewin, still on the sofa, but awake now and drinking coffee, listened. The Frenchman sang with taste and feeling, and Amy forgot, in the pleasure of the moment, that the polo match was probably over, and that Jack might appear suddenly and find her with Louvain. But the chiming of a little clock in the room reminded her of the lateness of the hour ; and rising abruptly from the piano, she was about, with some pretty excuse, to dismiss both her visitors, when the sound of a violent altercation, apparently on the lawn just outside the verandah, arrested her attention and that of her companions also.

"Are you mad?" It was Rossitur who spoke. "I will not let you go! You will kill her! You know you will!"

Lewin rushed out. Amy, white and trembling, clung to Louvain's arm.

"It is something about my husband!" she said.

CHAPTER V.

AT THE LYCH GATE.

SOME two or three weeks, perhaps, before the sudden and tragic death of young John Erskine at Simla, the village of Stillingfort, in Stoneshire, was *en fête* to celebrate the return of Lord and Lady Stillingfort and their daughter from a lengthened absence abroad. Her ladyship's health, it was said, obliged them to leave England the preceding winter, and they went away directly at the close of the season, without coming to Stillingfort Park even for a few months in the early autumn.

A short stay was made in London upon the return of the family from the South of France; and when it was announced that they were expected home, a rumour reached the village in advance of the engagement of the Earl's only daughter, Lady Judith, to an enormously rich and childless widower nearly double her age. He was a commoner, whose father had made his colossal fortune in trade; neither envy nor calumny could find one word to say against him, but he would not have been accepted by the proud Earl and Countess of Stillingfort for their daughter were it not for the princely settlement he proposed to make upon her.

The news of the engagement was widely circulated in the village, and created an unusual amount of excitement; for the attachment of the beautiful Lady Judith to Charles Rossitur, the farmer's son and organist of the parish church, was a sort of open secret in the neighbourhood. It was whispered how, last year when she was at home, she used, three or four times a week, to go to the church when she knew he would be found in

the organ loft pouring out his soul in music
at his beloved instrument.   But whether the
maiden of high degree and the poor musician,
whose handsome face and noble form had
attracted her notice, met as mere acquaintances who were interested in music, or as
lovers interested solely in themselves, no one
knew.   The poor old fellow who so patiently
blew for hours while Rossitur played, was
both blind and deaf, and if he had any suspicions as to the nature of the interruptions
that so often put an end to the organist's
daily practice, he never spoke of them to
anyone.   He was one of Lady Judith's
favourite pensioners, and she was very kind
to him.

Early in the afternoon of the day the
Stillingforts were expected home, Charles
Rossitur and his sister Alice were walking
together not fifty yards from the spot where
their sister Bella stood with Pottinger when
poor Jem Hathaway, her hoodwinked lover,

shot himself. Alice was in every way a remarkable contrast to her handsome sister and brother. She was a short, spare little woman, with scanty dark hair, and a sallow, sickly complexion, and in her eyes alone was any resemblance to be found to the handsome race from which she sprang. She was not specially amiable in mind or manner, and she had the reputation of being able, on occasion, to use a shrewish tongue with good effect.

If she loved any creature upon earth with a strong, unselfish love, it was her only brother, and, from the first, she had seen his wild infatuation for Lady Judith Forster with sorrow and dismay. No good, she knew, could ever come of such a love, and moreover, she did not believe in the sincerity of the high-born beauty. It was an immense relief to her when the family went abroad for an indefinite time, for she hoped her brother would shake off the glamour of Lady Judith's beauty, when he was no longer under its constant influence, and make up his mind that he could never win her for his wife. Before she had bewitched him the young man had been well inclined to a modest girl in his own station, and Alice looked back with infinite regret to the time he had walked in that very wood with herself and Ellen Balfour, the village schoolmistress, whose naturally beautiful voice had improved so much under his training that she had several times appeared at the local concerts.

Now, as far as Alice knew, he never spoke to her except in the most formal manner, and it was scarcely to be expected that the man who gave lessons to Lady Judith Foster, and sang his own songs in fine houses in London, would trouble himself about the insignificant person who taught the village children to read. As the brother and sister walked up and down the pretty woodland path, they naturally talked of what was uppermost in

their minds—the home-coming of the family
to the Park and the rumoured engagement
of Lady Judith.

"If it were announced in fifty newspapers
it is not true," Charles Rossitur said, doggedly.
"You may think I am boasting, Alice, if you
like, but she loves me and she will be true to
me in spite of everyone.   Do you suppose I
don't know?"

"I never said she did not love you, dear,"
the girl answered, in the slow quiet manner
peculiar to her, "but I say again, as I said to
you many times before, that she will never
marry you.   Her pride is far greater than her
love, and, besides, it is not as if she was rich.
She is a lord's daughter, but she has no
fortune, you know; and what have you to
offer her in comparison to this Mr. Milbanke?
He has about half-a-million a year, they say."

"And what is he with his half-million?   A
man nearly old enough to be her father."

"Age is nothing with such a fortune; you

haven't a farthing but your salary as organist
of the church, and what you make now and
then by writing a song.   There is the farm,
to be sure, when father dies; but do you
suppose his lordship would let you keep
that if you married his daughter against his
wish?"

"I can always sell my interest in it."

"And live on that!" cried Alice, scornfully.
"Why, your yearly income would not keep
your fine lady wife in gloves——"

"You do not know her noble heart,"
interrupted Rossitur, impetuously.   "If I
cannot get on in this country she will come
with me to America or Australia, and we can
face the world together."

"My poor brother!" said Alice.   "What
will become of you when your dream is
broken up?   Oh! if I could persuade you
that you are deceiving yourself about this
girl, and that she——"

"Listen to me," Rossitur interrupted again,

and stopping suddenly he put his hand on his sister's shoulder and looked into her face. "You ask what will become of me if Judith Forster plays me false. The bare idea of it turns my brain; so, if it happens, remember that whatever I do will be the act of a madman. May God help me, for I cannot answer for myself!"

"Oh, my brother!" and Alice, the cold, undemonstrative Alice, flung herself weeping on his breast. "I wish you had never seen her beautiful, false face. Forget her, dear. Do not let your life be blighted by this love. You are handsome and clever; there is not one of her fine friends, with their money and their titles, to be compared to you. Perhaps if she did not know you, or if her people did not know you, she might marry you; but look at me, with my hands all red and rough from common work at home. Look at our father; he can just make a shift to read and write—there was little schooling when he was young, and Bella, our sister, is a soldier's wife."

"It is of no use to talk in that way," the young man answered. "Judith loves me, and she is more to me than my life. And I shall see her presently," he added, his face flushing with rapture at the thought. "She will come to the church this evening if she can, I know she will; and if not to-day, then to-morrow. I shall see her. My beauty! my queen! Do not look so solemn, Alice. Treat me as a madman if you like, but you must laugh over my folly until we see who wins—the organist or the millionaire."

"I do not feel as if I should ever laugh again," she said.

"Nonsense, girl! Come along with me to the church gate and let us see the carriage go past from the station. The train is due in half-an-hour, and it will take us twenty minutes to walk down."

But Alice would not go.

"I do not want to see her," she said; "and the less she sees of your relations the better for you."

And if he had thought about making a good impression, Charles Rossitur could scarcely have been more picturesquely posed than he chanced to be when Lady Judith's eager, restless eyes caught sight of him, as, seated beside her mother in the open barouche, she dashed past the old church on her way from the station. He was leaning against the quaint old lych gate, and the dark back-ground might have been chosen by an artist, who wished to set off to advantage the handsome face with the dark, passionate eyes and the fair brown hair.

For one moment his glance met that of Lady Judith as he bared his head to salute the occupants of the carriage; to two of whom, it must be confessed, he was at that moment the must unwelcome sight in the world. Lord Stillingfort frowned, his wife looked at the young man without making the slightest sign of recognition, and Lady Judith, as she slightly bent her head, lowered her parasol to hide the burning blush that mounted to her face.

After many months of absence she saw him again ; and on her finger at that moment was the almost priceless diamond ring, the pledge of her engagement to Mr. Milbanke.

She had now to choose between the two ; and that evening Charles Rossitur's organ practice was not interrupted.

CHAPTER VI.

FACE TO FACE.

AND Lady Judith knew well enough that her young lover was waiting and watching and hoping for her coming, but she was not bold enough to run the risk of going to meet him on the very evening of her return. The suspicions of her father and her mother, which had been aroused before they left Stillingfort, would have been on the alert at once if she had gone out alone within an hour or two of her arrival at home ; and neither could she venture to send Charles Rossitur a note ; she had not a messenger whom she could trust.

Alice asked her brother no questions when he came home, looking sadly disappointed and in miserable spirits, from his evening practice at the church. "He was a fool to expect her," the girl said to herself.

The next morning the young man, after a sleepless night, was up and out wandering alone in the woods soon after daylight. It occurred to him that Lady Judith, on the chance of a meeting, might also come out for an early ramble; but not a soul was to be seen except a woodman going to his work or a gamekeeper returning from his rounds.

Rossitur was excited, jealous, and wild with the desire that possessed him to meet Judith face to face, and hear from her own lips that the report of her engagement was untrue; and wild also with his ardent longing to clasp her in his arms after their long separation, broken once only by a precious letter she had sent him early in the year. But she had desired him on no account to answer it, and he had obeyed. Night and day since he

received it, that letter had been his constant
companion, and he took it out now and read
it again as he walked up and down the woodland path, hoping at each turn to see her
coming towards him.

Before he went home to the early breakfast at the farm he had taken a mighty
resolve. He would go that very day to
Lord Stillingfort and ask him for his
daughter. It was the most honourable
and manly course to pursue, and if he
refused, as was but too probable, to listen
to the prayer of the poor and humble
suitor, Rossitur would consider himself free
to marry Lady Judith, if she loved him well
enough to brave poverty and estrangement
from her family and friends for his sake.

And, judging her by himself, he had no
fear. Had he been a peer's son and she the
farmer's daughter, he knew the difference in
rank would not keep him from her; but it did
not occur to him that the husband raises the

wife to his own social level, or pulls her down as the case may be.

When breakfast was over he told Alice that he might not be home in time for the early family dinner, as, after the choir practice, he was going to the Park to see Lord Stilling-fort on business.

"Oh, indeed!" she said ; "and you expect to be asked to luncheon, I suppose."

It was impossible to tell by her manner whether she spoke satirically or in earnest.

"I expect a great deal, I admit," he answered, with a smile, "but I do not know that I thought about luncheon. However, if I come home hungry, you will give me some food ?"

He kissed her and went out, and she stood for some time looking after him with tears in her eyes.

"It is madness!" she said to herself, "downright madness! If she would tell him herself that she is going to marry this rich man, he would be cured ; but she will keep him on and play with him until she breaks his heart."

It was still very early, not more than one o'clock, when Rossitur rang the great bell and asked the powdered and supercilious flunkey who answered it, and who knew him well by sight, if Lord Stillingfort was at home. He was shown into the library, and then, the footman, having announced the early visitor to his master, went back to the servants' hall and told his companions that " that 'ere horganist chap had called to see his lordship, and it was a wonder he 'ad n't come in the middle of the night."

Rossitur had to wait with what patience he could muster for nearly a quarter-of-an-hour before Lord Stillingfort appeared ; the fact was, that when he heard who was waiting for him he went off in a great hurry to his wife to beg of her to be present at the interview, but she refused. " I daresay he

wants money for the organ," she said. "Just
give him a cheque and send him away as
soon as possible."

"And suppose it is something about
Judith?"

At that Lady Stillingfort laughed. "If it
is," she said, "you can order him out of the
house. But I do not suppose he has lost his
senses, although he fancies himself in love
with her." Then as her husband was leaving
the room, she called him back and added,
"If he says anything about Judith, just send
for her and make her tell him before your face
that she is going to marry Mr. Milbanke.
How unfortunate that he had to go to
America just now. If he were but here we
might have the marriage directly."

Lord Stillingfort met his unwelcome visitor
with polite urbanity; but he contrived also to
make his greeting formal in the extreme.

"Good morning, Mr.—ah—yes—Rossitur,
to be sure, the organist. I did not quite

catch the name from Thomas. May I ask you to state your business as briefly as possible, as I am very busy this morning? After my long absence I have a great deal to look into. What can I do for you?"

He did not sit down or ask his visitor to be seated; so the young man stood, and he looked like a young giant beside the spare little man who stared at him so coldly through his gold-rimmed *pince-nez*.

"Lord Stillingfort," Rossitur began, and it must be confessed that the hopes which had buoyed him during his walk to the Park had all died away, "it is now nearly two years since I had the honour of giving your daughter, Lady Judith, some lessons on the organ, and I—since that time, I mean—that is I——"

"Oh; you mean, I suppose, the lessons were never paid for," interrupted Lord Stillingfort, brusquely. "Really, that was very remiss; but why didn't you send in your bill?

Then it would have been settled with the other accounts. What is the amount, and I'll write you a cheque at once !"

Rossitur's face grew scarlet. "Pardon me, my lord," he said. "It was an understood thing when I gave Lady Judith lessons that they were not to be paid for, and I am sorry you think I came here for money. My object is something very different. I came," and he raised his handsome head proudly, and looked Lord Stillingfort straight in the face, "I came to tell you that I love your daughter, and to ask your consent to our marriage."

Lord Stillingfort adjusted his *pince-nez* and stared in his turn at his audacious visitor.

"You love my daughter, and you ask my consent to your marriage with her!" he repeated. "Upon my word, young man, I must do you the justice to say that you are very frank, and apparently not much troubled by any doubts as to the success of your suit. When you talk of my consent you imply that you have already obtained that of Lady Judith. May I ask if this is so ?"

" I have every reason to hope that if your consent were obtained Lady Judith would become my wife."

" Do you know what, sir ?" his lordship broke in with a dry chuckle—he was too angry to laugh—" it would serve you right and teach you a timely lesson, if I were to ring the bell and order my servants to turn you out of the house ! Have you forgotten, sir," and his voice rose angrily, " who and what you are ? What right have you to come and ask for my daughter ? How dare you so much as think of her ? What is your position ? What are your means ? Your father is a tenant farmer on my estate, one of your sisters is in service, and you hold the not very lucrative post of organist of the parish church ! I have no wish to be unduly hard upon you, but your proposal is simply impertinent. And now, perhaps, the sooner you go the better," he added after a moment's pause, "and I must—"

"I cannot be dismissed in this way, my lord," broke in Rossitur, passionately. "I may not be the equal of your daughter in rank; but, although we are only tenant farmers, the Rossiturs are every whit as old a family as your own. For myself, I can say that the one talent I possess has already brought me some social distinction, and at the present day people do not ask questions about an artist's birth. I am not very rich, it is true, but I love your daughter, and I am willing to work for her with all the power of mind and body I possess. Cheered and encouraged by her love, I believe I can achieve greatness, and I am proud and happy to know that her love is mine."

Lord Stillingfort at these bold words fairly lost his temper, and in his passion he flung the papers that were strewn upon the library table about, and all but overturned an ink-stand.

"Your insolence passes all bounds, sir," he almost shouted. " Perhaps you are not aware that Lady Judith is engaged to be married, and that the husband she has chosen is one of whom we cordially approve."

" I heard a report of Lady Judith's engagement to a Mr. Milbanke," Rossitur replied, " but I do not believe it."

" Perhaps you do not believe *me*," Lord Stillingfort cried. "Very well." He rang the bell. " Tell Lady Judith to come to me at once," he said to the footman who answered it ; and not another word was spoken until the door opened and Lady Judith came hurriedly in.

When she saw who was in the room she stopped short ; the colour rushed to her face and then as quickly left it again.

"You sent for me, papa," she said. And

then she stood like a statue, with her eyes bent on the ground, and the man whose heart was breaking for a word or look from her, feasted his eyes for a few blissful moments upon her matchless beauty.

"Judith," said her father, "this young man, Rossitur, says he has heard a report that you are engaged to be married to Mr. Milbanke, and he does not believe it even when confirmed by me. Will you be kind enough to tell him whether it is true or not?"

Lady Judith gave one rapid glance at Rossitur; then her eyes fell again, and she was silent.

"Speak! I insist upon it!" cried her father. " Is it true or false that you wear his ring on this finger," and he took her left hand and held it up, "and that you have promised to marry him?"

" It is true," she answered, so low that Rossitur barely caught the words. Then she turned and rushed from the room.

" I hope you are satisfied," said Lord
Stillingfort.

But the young man's pale and quivering
lips could frame no reply.

CHAPTER VII.

TRUE OR FALSE.

WHEN he left the house, dumb with bitter disappointment, and his wounded pride stinging him sore, Rossitur struck across the Park towards the woods, intending to make his way back to the farm circuitously. The whole thing had been so sudden that he was bewildered and totally unable to realise that, from Judith's own lips, he had received the deathblow to all his hopes. There was the hateful ring glittering on her finger; what better evidence could he have of her perfidy, even if her own faltering admission of the truth had not been confirmed by her father's words?

He walked on in a stupid, blundering kind

of way until he reached a little glade, so shut
in and lonely that he knew he should be free
from observation ; and there, flinging himself
face downwards on the turf, he gave vent to
his passionate grief.   How long he lay there
he never knew ; it might have been for hours
or only minutes, for in his abandonment he
was quite lost to the passage of time.   But at
length he heard a light, quick step approaching, and presently someone knelt beside him
and a soft hand was passed over his hair.

"Look up !   Speak to me—to Judith,"
whispered the low, musical voice that had
been so hard and constrained when last he
heard it ; and instantly he sprang to his feet,
and she was by his side with her hands
clasped round his arm.

"Why did you say it ?" he cried.   " Did
you want to drive me mad ?   You told me
the truth just now, I suppose, and I do not
want to hear it again.   Take away your
hands.   I cannot answer for myself while

you stand there looking at me with those eyes."

" I take them away for this," she cried, and flung them round his neck. " Do you think I am going to give you up?" she murmured, and for answer he clasped her to his heart and kissed her as he had never dared to kiss her before.

" My love! my darling!" he said, passion-ately, " I cannot live without you!"

Then she told him how she had slipped out, when she knew her father and mother were shut up together, in the hope of in-tercepting him in the wood, and she gently upbraided him for having gone to her father at all.

" You knew he would never consent to our marriage," she said, "even if there were no Mr. Milbanke in the question. Perhaps if you were to write some grand opera, and get famous all at once, he might listen to you, but as you are now, you have no chance.

You do not mind my saying this, do you?"
she added, looking at him with admiring
eyes, "for you know I do not want you one
whit different from what you are."

He listened enraptured. The glamour of
her presence was too strong to leave any
room for reason or commonsense, and not
one thought was given by him to the future
as he stood beside her in that secluded spot.
It was enough for him that she had come to
him there of her own accord, and had allowed
him to clasp her in his arms and lavish upon
her a hundred endearing names. He, no
doubt, believed that she would give up her
rich lover for his sake, and abandon father,
mother and home at his bidding; but he
little knew the nature of the woman, who
certainly would have given all she possessed
in the world if she could have transferred the
money bags of Mr. Milbanke to this penniless
youth, whose noble beauty of face and grace
of figure would haunt her to her dying day.

The danger of the double game she was playing was patent enough to her; she looked ahead after every cautious or incautious move, but she trusted to the chapter of accidents to see her safely out of the mesh in which she had involved herself.   She knew perfectly well that marriage with Rossitur in his present position, or indeed in any position, was absolutely impossible, and that her marriage with Mr. Milbanke was an absolute certainty.   To love a poor man and to philander with him was one thing, to link herself voluntarily to his poverty was another.   But as the summer days sped on, and these stolen meetings in the wood were continued, she made much ado to persuade Rossitur that if he would but be patient all would be well. It would never do for them to run away on the chance of obtaining her father's forgiveness as soon as she was married.   The only way out of the difficulty was to temporise.

His proud spirit chafed against the secrecy,

but his infatuation, which day by day became wilder and less under control, forced him to bend to her will.

His sister Alice, watching him narrowly, saw that since the return of Lady Judith he had some secret spring of happiness to which he gave her no clue. He was in the gayest spirits; the light had come back to his eyes and the elasticity to his step. He once more took pleasure in his work, and it was at that time that one of the sweetest songs he ever composed was written and sent off to the publisher. Love inspired him, and he wrote as he had never written before.

What was the meaning of it all, the sister wondered. He still heard Lady Judith's engagement spoken of in the village; it was rumoured that Mr. Milbanke was expected immediately at the Park, and that as soon as he came the wedding-day would be fixed. Alice made up her mind to act the spy, and find out when and where her brother and

Lady Judith met, for that they met and met often, she was certain.

She noticed that four and sometimes five times a week he went out, always at the same hour, with a book under his arm, as if for a quiet saunter in the woods. She at first thought that Lady Judith would not be rash enough to meet him so near home, but still it was possible. So she followed him one afternoon, and was an eye-witness to the meeting between the lovers. It was ardent enough to imply not only devotion but constancy on both sides, but Alice could not and would not believe in the lady's sincerity ; so she made up her mind, at all hazards, to put an end to this clandestine intercourse.

Her first attempt was made with her brother.

" It is of no use to deny to me that you meet her," she said, " for I followed you yesterday to Warleigh Copse "—the sequestered glade in Stillingfort Wood that the

lovers had chosen for their trysting-place—
"and saw you together."

"I had no idea that I had a spy for a
sister," Rossitur broke in angrily.

"I spy upon you," she retorted, "because
you are laying up misery for yourself in the
future and behaving dishonourably now. I
suppose you are fond of that woman, and she
likes you well enough to meet you in secret;
but mark my words, she will never marry you,
and you ought to be too proud to let her
delude you into these underhand dealings.
If you were her equal in birth it would be
different, but your father's son cannot afford
to act dishonourably."

Rossitur winced. He had many scruples
about the deception he was carrying on, but
he silenced them all by the plea that he and
Lady Judith were driven to meet in secret,
as her father had practically turned him out
of the house and insulted him by asking if he
had come for money. But then the temp-

tation ! He was young ; he was in love, and willing to fling everything to the winds for her sake.

" Do you suppose I don't know all that ?" he exclaimed ; " but a man must fight with the best weapons he has. Lord and Lady Stillingfort are bent upon forcing their daughter into a marriage she abhors ; she is obliged to temporise to protect herself, and it would be hard indeed if we were never to meet."

Alice said no more, but an anonymous communication which reached Lord Stillingfort the following day was written by her. It briefly informed his lordship that Lady Judith and Charles Rossitur, the organist, were in the habit of meeting almost every day at a certain hour in Warleigh Copse, in the heart of Stillingfort Wood.

" It is a curious revenge of fate," Lord Stillingfort said to himself, as, having ascertained that his daughter was not in the house, he set out for Warleigh Copse to interrupt the lovers' meeting. "When this young fellow was an infant, my stepbrother carried off his mother from her husband, and now the child is a man, and he makes secret love to my daughter. Were it not for the horrible wrong his family had suffered from a member of mine it would go hard with him to-day; but, knowing what I do, how can I accuse him of dishonour?"

Disheartened by his sister's reproaches, Rossitur that same afternoon urged upon Lady Judith the necessity of making it known without further delay that she did not mean to fulfil her engagement with Mr. Milbanke.

"Every day you grow dearer and more dear to me, my darling," he said, "and every day I hate more and more the false position I am in."

"I am glad you have the grace to acknowledge that the position is a false one," said the sharp clear voice of Lord Stillingfort at his elbow—so absorbed were the lovers in one another that he came upon them un-observed—" and, therefore, the sooner it is put an end to finally the better."

Rossitur fell back mortified beyond expression, and unable for very shame to utter a word in his defence as the angry father drew his daughter's arm within his own. Then the thought that his too brief hours of happiness were over, and that long months, if not years, of weary waiting might be before him and the woman who was so madly beloved, overcame him, and he eagerly, passionately entreated to be allowed one word of farewell.

But Lord Stillingfort was inexorable. " I cannot trust my daughter out of my sight," he said, with a glance at her that said more than words ; but, for some reason known only to himself, he did not reproach the young man.

" You must not blame her, my lord," cried

Rossitur, " I am in fault throughout. I urged her to meet me here secretly. I beseech you do not visit my wrong-doing upon her."

Lord Stillingfort, who had turned away, stopped short, and faced Rossitur again. " Judith," he said, addressing his daughter, " Is what he says true? Did he ask you to meet him here?"

She raised her beautiful eyes to the young man's face, hesitated for a moment, and then answered, boldly, " Yes, papa."

It was but the corroboration of his own statement, but, somehow, the falsehood that had fallen so glibly from her lips sent a deadly chill of disappointment through him and planted the first doubt in his heart.

Was the woman who had uttered it herself true or false?

CHAPTER VIII.

MRS. ERSKINE FORECASTS THE FUTURE.

I⊤ was all over! The tragedy, so awful in its suddenness, which had left Amy Erskine a widow and her infant son heir to the old title and estates, was already, although barely a month had passed, almost forgotten in Simla, and life there went on as before. Nothing came out respecting the communication that was handed to the unfortunate young man just before the last game of polo began; and the impression that his reckless play had been caused by some information conveyed to him by the few lines the note contained died out at once as soon as his servant declared that the handwriting was that of Mrs. Erskine.

No one supposed that she had any news of an exciting or agitating nature to communicate, and not even the most censorious gossip could make anything out of the fact that when Pottinger, the dead man's soldier-servant, arrived from the polo ground in a high state of excitement with the news of his master's death, Mrs. Erskine had two visitors, gentlemen, with her. She was pretty and popular, and not a day passed without bringing visitors to the bungalow and poor Gus Lewin — a good - natured creature as everyone knew—had been most kind and efficient. He had broken the awful news to the poor young widow, and when she was sitting there in a sort of stupor, dazed by the sudden shock, it was Gus who thought of fetching the little boy to see if the sight of him would rouse her.

Victor de Louvain's name was seemingly not mentioned by anyone ; it was really his ready arm that caught and supported Mrs.

Erskine when, on hearing from Captain
Lewin—who, with the greatest difficulty, had
with Rossitur's help succeeded in keeping
Pottinger out of the room—that " Jack " had
met with a bad accident, she had reeled back
and all but fainted ; but, before she recovered
full consciousness, he had disappeared from
the scene.   No one spoke of him as having
been an eye-witness to the young widow's
reception of the terrible news and no one
but Rossitur knew how the dead man had
hated him.   She, putting always the worst
construction upon the action of her employers,
would have been the last to admit that the
jealousy of the husband was founded entirely
on the fact that the Frenchman had been
Amy's lover before her marriage.   Until that
fatal afternoon they had not met since Amy
became Mrs. Erskine ; neither had they held
any communication by letter.

As so often happens, poor young Erskine's
death was but the beginning of misfortunes.

Pottinger, whose brain had been more or less affected since a severe sunstroke the previous year, went clean out of his mind before his young master was buried, and was removed under restraint and finally sent to England and placed in an asylum for treatment; but the medical men who saw him before he started gave hopes of his ultimate recovery, and these hopes were, as a matter of course, communicated to his wife.

During the first few hours that passed after his return to the bungalow from the polo ground, he lay tossing about on his bed, and Rossitur, who seemed, when she chose to use it, to possess some magnetic influence over him, gathered from his low and often incoherent mutterings that he had either heard of, or seen, the note she had sent to his master. She had ascertained beyond all doubt that it was not on the dead man's person when he was brought home; but she knew that the utmost caution would be necessary if she attempted to search for it in her husband's pockets.

As night came on he grew rapidly worse, and before morning broke it took the united strength of three men to hold him, while he shouted furiously that his master was being murdered by that "devil;" and all the while he raved his wild eyes were fixed upon Bella's white, determined face! But she did not care now what he said in his delirium. She had found her letter in one of his pockets, and it was destroyed beyond all possibility or chance of resuscitation, so she could afford to ridicule his frantic words, and his agonised appeals for justice upon those who had "murdered his dear master."

He got perceptibly calmer when his wife, who cerainly had not been watching him from affection, and who, now that her object was attained, made no attempt to soothe him, left him to the care of others ; nor did she, it may be added,take any further trouble about him during the short time he remained at the bungalow.

It was quite touching to see how her mistress turned to her for consolation and advice in her bereavement. Amy had never really domineered over anyone except her too indulgent husband ; she, herself, had always been like wax in the hands of her clever and unscrupulous maid, and it was Rossitur who was her most trusted adviser. It was Rossitur who instructed Captain Lewin how to address and word the telegram that was to convey the tragic news to the family at the Chase ; it was Rossitur who urged her bewildered mistress to dictate the few incoherent lines written by the maid in her own fine bold hand, and signed as boldly, " Your afflicted daughter, Amy Erskine," which left India for Stoneshire by the very mail, respecting the departure of which the husband and wife had talked an hour or two before the death of the former on

the polo ground.   And in that short epistle,
Mrs. Erskine, or Rossitur for her, promised
to write again more fully when she had
recovered somewhat from the terrible shock!

And it was Rossitur who saw the visitors
who came to inquire for Mrs. Erskine ; and
she also designed the monument that was
erected over her late master's grave, and the
inscription upon it was really her composition,
although she so cleverly contrived to put her
own words into the mouth of her mistress,
that Amy thought the graceful and touching
tribute to her husband's memory was all her
own.   Letters of condolence too, were, for
the most part, answered by Rossitur ; sometimes in the name of the widow, but as often
in her own ; there was but one, and one only,
that Amy kept to herself—but Rossitur contrived to get a peep at it—and answered with
her own hand, and that was a brief note of
manly unaffected sympathy from Monsieur de
Louvain, written from Calcutta.

He was about to start immediately for Europe, and any communication addressed to him, "Poste Restante, Naples," would find him up to a given time. There was not a word in the letter that might not have been printed and published to the world, but, somehow, Amy could not bring herself to treat a letter from him as she would have treated a letter from Gus Lewin, or any of her acquaintances in poor Jack's old regiment. She felt as if she owed him some compensation for the dead man's unreasonable aversion to him; and to herself also, just to prove, as it were, that the friendship between her and de Louvain was beyond reproach.

Poor Amy was perplexed beyond measure just then at the complication in her feelings. Her husband's sudden death had given her a terrible shock, and she most sincerely regretted that on that fatal afternoon she had let him go without a tender and wife-like farewell! Rather with a gibe indeed, which was meant in jest, but which was not pleasant to remember when he was brought home to her, dead.

It is not too much to say that she missed him at every turn. He had petted and spoiled her so persistently that she felt lonely without the attentions which had somehow bored her not a little when they were offered. Her social position, too, was now completely altered. Her baby boy might be Sir John some day, but she could never be Lady Erskine ; and although, no doubt, her father-in-law would give her a handsome allowance, in addition to her post - nuptial settlement, and a home at the Chase, she did not look forward to life in a dull English house in the country with much satisfaction.

So, although she grieved for her husband, she was by no means broken-hearted at his loss ; perhaps she was even more genuinely sorry for herself, and for all the trouble and discomfort her widowhood had brought her, than for the man who had loved her but too well.

Part of her trouble was caused by Pottinger's insanity. It was very inconsiderate of him, she thought, to go mad just as she particularly wanted him to have all his wits about him for her benefit and at her disposal. She could have bought his discharge from the regiment, and then he would have travelled home with her and Rossitur and the two children, and finally settled in England with his wife and their boy. But, as he had gone out of his mind, it was clearly her duty to keep Rossitur and her son until he recovered ; and, if he never recovered, Sir John, no doubt, would be able to get the child into an Orphan Asylum, and Rossitur would continue to act as her maid.

Thus did Amy Erskine forecast the future.

CHAPTER IX.

MISS MASHAM HAS HER SUSPICIONS.

"AND so he is back again from America? That is good news, so far." The speaker was little Miss Masham. She was in her own drawing-room at the Rosary, and the visitor she addressed was Letty Erskine, or Mrs. Herbert Otway, as she had a right to be called, and as she was always called in Little Centre Bridge. It was true, and known to everyone in town, that she and her husband had parted at the church door, so to speak but the marriage had not been annulled, and to all intents and purposes the pair were man and wife, although they never met, never wrote to one another, and, for what outsiders knew, never thought of one another.

But as to the thinking, only Otway for himself, and Letty for herself, could speak. But it is a fact that she believed firmly he had forgotten her, and he had no reason to think that the girl who had behaved so heartlessly to him on her wedding-day had fallen desperately in love with him three days later, and would have sacrificed everything she possessed — except her stubborn pride, of course—to hear him say once more " Letty, I love you."

In many respects she was very much altered since the day, now more than a year ago, that she and her husband of an hour had stood face to face in the drawing-room in Halkin Street. In person she was more attractive ; her saucy, sparkling, girlish beauty had gained some quality impossible to define in words ; her pretty, slender figure had filled out and matured without the loss of an iota of her girlish grace, and if more silent and thoughtful than of old, she spoke

to more purpose now than in the old days
when thoughtless words and gay repartee fell
in one continuous stream from her pretty lips.

She could not in the least understand
herself how such a change had come over
her since she began to love the man whose
affection she had scorned and repulsed ; it
seemed now that to think of him, and to
live over again in memory the days she had
spent with him during their engagement,
made up the happiness of her life !   How
kind he had been !   How tender ; how indulgent to her absurd caprices ;   how patient,
and oh, how loving !   And how had she
repaid him ?   With stupid sarcasms she
was ashamed to remember ;   with coldness
—with indifference, and too often with unwomanly displays of petulance and temper !
Oh, for the power to live that year over
again ; to undo all that she had done, and
bind to her for ever and ever the one man
in the world whom she could honour as well

as love! That was how she put it; she was now as prone to exalt him unduly as, in her blindness, she had debased him.

But, cherished in secret, it was but natural that her repentance and love should grow, the one more absorbing, the other more painful in depth and sincerity. No one suspected what was going on in her mind, for the passion of pride was almost as strong as the love and repentance put together. Remembering Otway's outspoken scorn on the day of their final separation, she would have died rather than approach him as a suppliant for love and forgiveness.

Her father and aunt, who had at first taken the matter very much to heart, were now resigned to what appeared inevitable. They had outlived the awkwardness of having to explain that Letty and her husband had parted on their wedding-day, and that there was no hope of a reconciliation; and she lived on quietly at the Chase, and might have taken up her old life and been happy enough but for the cruel pain at her heart and the daily renewed and fierce struggle, which always ended in the same way, between love and pride.

Letty had always liked Miss Masham, but of late the two had become very fast friends indeed. The reason was not hard to find; the old lady was the only one who ever spoke to her of Otway. What she said was not always pleasant to hear, but Letty would have endured more disagreeable words for the satisfaction of hearing his name. She kept her secret most jealously guarded from this candid and clear-sighted friend, but nevertheless, Miss Masham suspected that Letty was less indifferent than she seemed, although to her the girl always dwelt upon Otway's declaration that his bride's treatment of him had given the death - blow to his affection for her.

" He is not the man I take him for, if it

would do anything of the kind," the old lady
used to say to herself; "but at the same
time, if women are capricious, men are fickle,
and it may be 'out of sight out of mind' with
him."

On this particular afternoon, Letty had
walked over to the Rosary to spend an hour
or two with her old friend, and her pony
carriage was to call for her about six o'clock.
Miss Masham was full of the news of Lady
Judith Forster's approaching marriage to Mr.
Milbanke, which she had heard that morning
from Dr. Murray, and he had had his information direct from Lord Stillingfort himself.

"And from what the doctor tells me, my
dear," she said, "I am afraid they have had a
great deal of trouble on account of that handsome young organist Charles Rossitur. It
seems he went to Lord Stillingfort and
proposed in form for the young lady, and then
it was found out that she and he used to
meet four or five times a week in the woods."

"I think it is very wrong to force her to marry Mr. Milbanke if she cares for Charles Rossitur," said Letty.

"Dear me! are you coming out as an advocate of romance?" cried Miss Masham.

"And why should I not?" asked Letty, quickly. "Are not all women romantic? I believe Judith cares for young Rossitur; why, then, should not Lord Stillingfort do something for him and let them marry?"

"Because, my dear, in the first place, the Stillingforts are as proud as Lucifer, and they do not believe that 'rank is but the guinea stamp,' unless the commoner has plenty of stamped guineas; and, in the second, because I believe that Lady Judith herself does not love this youth enough to give up position and money for his sake."

"A woman ought to give up everything in the world for the man she loves."

"Dear me! now, is that so?" said Miss Masham, with her little head on one side like a pert bird. "I thought love had gone out of fashion ages and ages ago. But, no doubt, you know more about it than I do."

"Indeed I do not. I never was in love, and I never mean to be."

"That being the case, it is a pity you happen to be married." And then came the abrupt remark: "And so he is back from America?"

"If you are speaking of Mr. Otway, I believe he came back from Florida a fortnight ago."

"And is there any chance of our seeing him down here? He is a man we all like very much—at least, I can speak for myself."

"I should think Little Centre Bridge is about the last place in England he would come to."

"That is strange, too, considering that his wife lives here."

"Now, Miss Masham, you know perfectly

well that he and I would go a hundred miles out of our way to avoid one another."

" I know nothing of the kind ; and I think if you did you would take a great deal of unnecessary exercise. I believe if you were to write to-day and say, 'Herbert, come ;' he would telegraph to say, 'Letty, I am coming ;' and when you met you would rush into one another's arms !"

" I am quite sure I shouldn't rush into his."

" But if he rushed into yours it would do just as well."

Letty shook her head.

" Then, my dear girl, if you do not love Herbert Otway—and if I were a young lady and married to him I should simply adore such a nice, handsome fellow—it is your duty to have the marriage annulled, and to marry someone else, and to allow him to marry, too."

" I do not want to marry anyone."

" But he may have fallen in love with some
girl he met in America. You can't tell. The
American women are very fascinating, and it
is a shame to keep him gagged and bound
when you do not want him yourself."

" I do not want to keep him, I assure
you," Letty answered, with some asperity.
" He may marry a dozen American women,
each one more fascinating than the other,
if he likes."

" I have no doubt one would satisfy him
but he ought to be free to choose. What in
the world is the matter with the child now ?"

Letty's face had flushed suddenly from
chin to brow, and as suddenly the colour all
faded away again, leaving her as white as a
ghost.

" Look ! look ! Miss Masham," she cried.
" Do you see who is coming up the drive ?"

Miss Masham ran to the window and
looked out.

" Herbert Otway himself," she exclaimed.

"Now, Letty, faint in his arms, and everything will come right."

But Letty drew herself up stiffly. "I am not going to meet him," she said.

CHAPTER X.

THE BEARER OF BAD NEWS.

" BUT I do not see how you are to avoid
meeting him, my dear," said Miss Masham,
"unless you jump out of the window ; for you
must run against him in the hall if you go
that way. I know the door leading from the
conservatory is locked, and — here he is,"
as the door was opened and the parlour-
maid announced " Mr. Herbert Otway, from
London."

If Letty had been taken aback when she
recognised her husband—the man whom for
months past she had been pining to catch
even a passing glimpse of—in the unexpected
visitor, Otway was no less dumbfoundered
when, on entering Miss Masham's drawing-

room, he saw his wife—the girl still so
passionately loved in spite of all the determined efforts he had made to forget her, and
to take up some absorbing work in which he
could lose himself gladly, and so prevent his
mind from dwelling upon the happiness he
had lost.

But the joy that thrilled through him at
the mere sight of her, more beautiful, if
possible, than when she repelled and mocked
him on their wedding-day, was not visible in
his face ; and the bow with which he returned
her stiff salutation, was as unbending and
formal as her own.

" Mercy on me, what extraordinary polite-
ness," thought Miss Masham, but it struck
her that Otway looked both sad and serious,
and she suspected that his visit had some
serious import.

And she was right. An intimate friend of
his had heard of Jack Erskine's death, in a
private telegram from India, and he had come

down at once to break the sad news to the family at the Chase. He thought it more than probable that they would hear it first through the *Times* on the following Monday morning, unless it occurred to the widow, or some of her friends, to send a telegram. It did occur to them a few days after the accident happened, and at that very moment the message was near its destination.

Otway's courage failed him completely as soon as he reached Little Centre Bridge station. How could he face Sir John with the appalling news of his son's death? How could he stand face to face with Letty in the first great sorrow of her life without betraying that his love for her was not dead, and so expose himseif to another rebuff?

Then he thought of kind little Miss Masham. He would go to her in the first instance, tell her what had happened, and consult with her upon the best means of breaking the news to the bereaved father.

That he might come across Letty, or any of the family at the Rosary, never occurred to him, and never in his life had he felt so embarrassed, or so utterly unable to decide quickly what to do, as when he found the woman who was his wife, and yet not his wife, seated with their common friend.

Miss Masham saw at once there was something wrong. " I am very glad to see you, Mr. Otway," she said, and she spoke in her most matter-of-fact tone. " Strange to say, I was just asking Letty if you were back from America. It is very nice of you to come first to me, but——"

He interrupted her with a gesture. " I hoped to see you alone," he said, " for I am sorry to say I am the bearer of bad news——"

Letty rose hurriedly ; he had glanced at her as he spoke. " Not from India ?" she said. " Is there anything wrong with Jack or Amy ?"

She was close to him now; her face was
still very white, and her hand was laid with a
nervous clasp on Miss Masham's arm. "You
will think me very silly, I dare say," she went
on, "but for a week past I have been expecting to hear bad news.   I never mentioned it
to anyone for fear of being laughed at, but
twice lately I distinctly saw Jack lying on the
ground as if he were dead, with a crowd of
men about him.   "Has anything happened
to him?"

"He met with an accident playing polo a
few days ago," Otway answered, "and he
is——"

"Dead!" cried Letty.   "Oh! I knew it!
I knew it!   Oh! poor papa!"

She was swaying on her feet, overcome by
sudden faintness.   Otway sprang forward and
caught her in his arms; but either she had
her senses sufficiently about her to recoil a
little when he touched her, or he fancied she
did, for he at once overcame his first impulse

to hold her while he sent Miss Masham for
restoratives, and half-leading, half-supporting
her to the nearest couch, he laid her gently
down and then stood aside.

She had not actually fainted, and a sigh
broke from her involuntarily as she thought
how irksome it must have been to him to be
obliged to do anything for her; he had got
rid of her so quickly.

" I am better," she said, presently.   Then
she turned her face away and burst into tears.
Some of them were shed for the dead
brother, but those that were wrung from her
by the too evident coldness and indifference
of the man who had once loved her so well,
were a hundred-fold more full of anguish and
heartfelt grief!   And how carefully it behoved
her now to guard the secret of her love.

As she wept silently, Miss Masham and
Otway talked together, and he told her all
he knew of the accident.   But no particulars
had reached him; the telegram to his friend

had simply mentioned the accident at the polo match. "Of course, Mrs. Erskine will write, or someone for her," he said; "she must have plenty of friends out there. At Simla I think it happened."

"Yes; they went to Simla with the Viceroy," Letty said, rousing herself with an effort and sitting up. Otway involuntarily glanced at her left hand as she put both up to fasten a loose lock of hair, and saw the wedding-ring, with its keeper, on her finger.

"Her badge of servitude, poor girl!" he said to himself with bitter emphasis. "How she must hate to look at it!"

"It will break papa's heart!" Letty went on. "He was fonder of Jack than of anyone in the world! Oh! I hope Amy will come home at once and bring the boy. He will be a comfort to us and papa will like to bring him up at the Chase. "I suppose," and she glanced at Otway—he thought her

quickly averted look meant repugnance —
"you heard nothing of my sister-in-law?"

"There was nothing about Mrs. Erskine
in the telegram; but excuse me for suggest-
ing, do you not think it would be well to
break the news to Sir John and Miss
Lambton? A telegram might arrive from
Simla at any moment."

"Oh, certainly!" cried Letty, rising quickly.
"Thank you for reminding me. Has the
carriage come, Miss Masham?"

Otway went to the window, and saw his
old friends, Fire and Smoke, the ponies,
stamping and tossing their pretty heads
about at the door. The mere sight of the
handsome tricky little pair in their bright
harness brought with it such a train of
recollections, that for a few seconds he could
not speak. Then he said, with perfect composure, "Yes; your ponies are here."

"He forgets the drives we used to take
together!" thought Letty. "I wonder if he

remembers even their names!" She threw
her arms round Miss Masham's neck for a
moment, and hid her face on the kind little
woman's shoulders. "Oh! it is hard to
bear!" she sobbed, "so hard!"

"It is, my dear; very, very hard! But
you must not cry;" and she patted the
girl's shoulder in a tender, motherly fashion.
Otway turned away; what right had he to
witness the grief he could not soothe?

"Now if I could send them off together
something might come of it;" thought Miss
Masham, as Letty put on her hat and gloves
and once more said good-bye.

"Come over to-morrow," the girl said.

"Yes, dear, yes; good-bye. Don't fret too
much. Mr. Otway, will you see Miss——I
mean Mrs.——that is, will you see *Letty* to
the carriage."

He put her in and she tried to take the
reins; but her hands trembled so violently
she could not hold them, and she was blinded

by the tears that were streaming behind her veil.

"You are not fit to drive or to go alone," he cried. "Take the other seat and give me the reins."

The authoritative voice, and the determined gesture with which he took the whip and reins acted like a charm. She moved meekly without a word, and left the driving seat empty; he stepped in, and to her infinite surprise and pleasure, Miss Masham saw the pair drive off together.

But the not very long distance between the Rosary and the Chase was traversed in complete silence. Letty could not speak, Otway would not; and he looked cold, stern and forbidding enough to frighten any timid and shrinking woman as he whipped the ponies at a smart pace through the town.

Mrs. Crump's was full of ladies shopping, and for half-an-hour after the carriage passed a hot argument was carried on as to who the man was who was driving Mrs. Otway!

Letty jumped out as the ponies stopped; the great door stood open as usual, and she ran into the hall. The house seemed unusually silent; Miss Lambton and Orion generally appeared to welcome Letty when she came back from her drives, but this afternoon there was not a sound; not even the welcoming bark of a dog.

"Perhaps papa and Aunt Louise are out," she said to Otway, who was following her. She looked into the drawing-room; it was empty; so also was the morning-room. She went on to the library, and softly opening the door, looked in. One glance was enough to tell her that the terrible blow she hoped to avert had fallen in her absence. Sir John was seated at the table with his face buried in his hands. The telegram from India was on the floor by his side, and Miss Lambton, in a chair close by, was gazing at him mournfully, and every now and then putting her handkerchief to her eyes.

Letty rushed forward and threw her arms round her father's neck! At her touch the old man turned, and, hiding his face upon her bosom, sobbed out, "Oh, Letty, my darling, I have lost my boy!"

CHAPTER XI.

FATHER AND DAUGHTER.

It was some time before Letty could soothe poor Sir John's outburst of grief. The news was so unexpected, and was conveyed to him with such concise coldness by the telegram, that he was utterly prostrated by the shock. But at length Letty's gentle caresses and loving care brought him round, and he lay on a couch in the library, and, with her hand in his, talked quietly and naturally of his lost son.

" But how did you hear the news, my darling ?" he said at last. " Surely it is not known in the town yet ?"

" No, papa." And Letty hesitated and blushed painfully ; it cost her so much to speak of Otway, and yet speak of him she must sooner or later. " I heard it from Mr. Otway."

" From Otway ! Do you mean Herbert Otway, the man you married?" and Sir John, in his amazement, sat up and stared at his daughter. " Did he send you the news ?"

" He did not send it, papa. He came down himself to break it to us. It was mentioned in a telegram sent to a friend of his. He did not like to come here, so he went to the Rosary, and I was there with Miss Masham——"

" And you met !" interrupted Sir John. " Well ; and what happened ?"

" Nothing happened," answered Letty. " He drove me home, and he is here now."

" And do you mean to tell me you never spoke to one another—that you have not made it up ?"

" I do not think we even shook hands,"

said Letty. "Indeed I am sure we did not; and as to making up, as you call it, it is impossible! You know how I dislike him, papa, and I should think he is now quite indifferent to me; his manner certainly implied as much."

Sir John sighed. "It is very odd," he said; "a pretty girl like you, and a fine, handsome fellow like Otway, and, although you are actually married to one another, you detest him, and he seems to have got over any liking he had for you! What do you think, Letty—has he got over it?"

"I should say he has quite got over it," replied Letty, promptly.

"Then I think something ought to be done to set you both free," said Sir John. "I know from what my poor dear boy said more than once in his letters to me, that *he* thought it was an awkward position for you to be in; and, perhaps, now that Otway is here it would be well to arrange with him to

have the marriage declared null and void.
What do you say?"

"It will be very disagreeable to me to have
the subject mentioned," said Letty, and with
great difficulty she controlled her trembling
voice. "If he wishes to be unmarried, let
him say so; I—I do not care about it one
way or the other."

"But you will care very much some day
when you meet a man you like and who
likes you. There was young Harry Digby
last winter would have given the world to
marry you! He thought you were a young
widow, and I had to explain to him how it
was. He asked me why I did not annul the
marriage, and said it could be done quite
easily."

"If it were annulled to-morrow," cried
Letty, "it would not help him, and I think
he was very impertinent to dictate to you!
I would not marry him if he were the only
man in the world!"

"Then Colonel Probyn was very much smitten with you! Surely you like him?"

"Yes; I like him, but I do not want to marry him."

"You must be very hard to please. Why can you not make friends with Otway and have done with it?"

"It is not of the slightest use to talk to me about *him*, papa ; and he cares quite as little for me as I care for him. Please do not let us talk about it any more ; we have so much to think of. I cannot believe that our darling Jack is dead ! Oh, how I wish he had never gone to India! Poor Amy ! What a terrible shock to her ! I wonder how she is."

"Ah! poor child! We must get her home at once with the boy. This is the proper place for them. She must live with us, poor darling! What a sad home-coming! And next year he was coming back on long leave, so proud, poor lad, with his wife and child !

But we must have her here as soon as she can come.   Eh, Letty?"

"Certainly she must come to us, papa.   I am sure she does not wish to stay in India, and your grandson ought to be brought up at the Chase.   Amy may marry again some day; but she ought to leave the boy with us."

"Marry again!" cried Sir John.   "Why should she marry again?   You are very good at marrying other people, my dear.   It will disappoint me very much if my son's widow marries again."

"But she is so young, papa."

"Her age has nothing to do with it.   Mrs. John Erskine can take a very good position in the county.   But if she chooses to marry, she must certainly leave the child with me; I am not going to give him up to the tender mercies of a stepfather!   Oh, poor Jack!   My poor, dear lad!   To think that you are dead!   I wonder if poor, dear Amy will be able to write and give us some particulars."

"She has never written to any of us," said Letty.

"But she will now; I am sure she will; and we must write by next mail and urge her to come home to us at once. What has become of your aunt? She was here when you came in."

"She is entertaining Mr. Otway, I suppose. I told you he was here."

"Here! in the house? He's not gone then? How very awkward! Is he going to stay, do you know?"

"He must stay to-night, I suppose," said Letty; "but I should think he will go away very early to-morrow morning."

"Oh, he had much better stay a day or two now he is here, and cheer us up a bit! That is, if you do not mind, my dear."

"It is a matter of perfect indifference to me," Letty answered; and as she spoke her heart was beating wildly at the bare idea of being in the same house with him for a few days.

"Then I shall ask him," said Sir John, "and before he goes we might, perhaps, be able to arrange something about annulling the marriage. I mean, of course, that *he* may make some proposition to me; and now, do you mind asking him to come and talk to me here for a while?"

Letty went without alacrity, and she found Otway with Miss Lambton. "Papa would like to see you," she said, halting just inside the door and not addressing anyone in particular.

Otway smiled; a most aggravating and impertinent smile, Letty thought. "To which of us does 'you' apply?" he said.

"Does Sir John want to see me, my dear?" Miss Lambton cried in the same breath.

"He wants to see Mr. Otway," Letty explained, speaking stiffly, with her head in the air.

"I am at his service," Otway answered, pleasantly.

As he passed Letty in the doorway she and he exchanged their first direct look that day. Her glance was cold and slightly scornful and defiant! His was an enigma! There was no warmth in it certainly, but there was neither scorn nor defiance; it would have taken an expert in eye language to read it aright; and even if Letty had been an expert she was by no means calm enough for analysis.

"How well he is looking!" Miss Lambton said, as soon as she and her niece were alone, "and he spoke so nicely and feelingly of darling Jack! And to think that they never met! It was so odd his meeting you at the Rosary, was it not? He told me all about it. I asked him how he thought you were looking, and he said he really hadn't noticed. If I did not know by experience how very truthful he is I should

not have believed him ; should you, my
dear ?"

" But, my dear aunt, you forget that he
and I find no pleasure in looking at one
another."

" Yes, dear ; I know you dislike him, but I
thought he liked you."

" Oh !" said Letty, and she laughed a
rather hard little laugh, " that was more than
a year ago."

CHAPTER XII.

OTWAY SAYS GOOD-BYE.

MISS MASHAM'S friends at the Rectory had an early visit from her the following day. " And were you not surprised to hear that Herbert Otway had come down?" she said, as soon as poor Jack Erskine's sudden death had been fully discussed. " I was never more astonished in my life than when he walked in ! And there was Letty as red as a peony, and looking—— I don't very well know what she looked like, except very pretty ! Half-angry and half-frightened, but if I am not very much mistaken, not altogether ill-pleased to see him again."

" But not exactly glad, I am afraid," said the doctor. " I ventured to talk to her

about him the other day, and to give her a
little bit of friendly advice about the
anomalous position they are both in, and she
fired up and asked me if I wanted her to live
with a man she detested—that was the word
—so what could I say ?"

" I have my suspicions about the detesta-
tion," said Miss Masham, " but, of course,
I may be wrong. One thing, however, is
certain; the first move must be made by
him. She will not stir a step, and to tell
you the truth, I do not see how she can."

" He was desperately in love with her,"
said the Rector. " I wonder if he has got
over it by this."

" He showed no signs of desperation yesterday!" said Miss Masham. "If she was
cool, he was cooler; but he drove her home
in the pony carriage from my house."

"I saw them," said Mrs. Murray. " I was
in Crump's, and I was certain the man who
was driving the ponies was Mr. Otway;

but when I said so, Mrs. Sumner and Mrs.
Verity, who happened to be in the shop too,
contradicted me flatly, and said they were
sure nothing would induce him to come here.

" Well ; you can have a crow over both of
them now, my dear," said the doctor, " for
you see he is here."

" I want to know if they will have to be
married over again if they are reconciled
now," said Miss Masham. "What do you
say, doctor?"

" Oh, dear, no ! The ecclesiastical cement
does not rub off like that. I am surprised
Sir John does not get the marriage annulled.
He told me himself that young Digby
proposed for Letty last winter, under the
impression that she was a widow."

"And that Colonel someone, who was
staying at the Chase in the spring, was very
much in love with her, Louise Lambton told
me. Well—who knows what will happen
now that they have met again ? But is it not

sad about young John ? To be killed playing polo! Poor fellow! I suppose the widow will come home at once with the——" but there Miss Masham stopped short.

Mrs. Murray had lost her baby boy when he was just a month old, and she had not as yet fully recovered her spirits.

"Sir John will not be happy without his grandson, we may be quite sure on that point," Dr. Murray said, quietly, "and we will all be glad to see the little man. Eh, Mary ?" with a fond glance at his wife. "By the way, I am curious to know if the wonderful maid will come here with Mrs. John Erskine. I should like to see if she is like her brother."

"That reminds me," said Miss Masham, "I have not seen either of you since your visit to Stillingfort Park. Has the millionaire lover arrived, and when is the wedding to be ?"

"In October, I believe ; but it may be

put off until after Christmas. We saw the millionaire's photograph; you must ask Mary what she thinks of it."

"I did not admire him particularly," Mrs. Murray answered, "but Lady Stillingfort assured me he has a very taking face. He looks tall and thin, and much too old for Lady Judith."

"How unfortunate!" said Miss Masham, "for young Rossitur, the organist, is so handsome, you tell me."

"Lord Stillingfort told me that Rossitur actually proposed to him for Lady Judith; and that after he sent him about his business she used to meet him in the woods every day! They telegraphed to America for Milbanke, and the young lady is closely watched for fear she should run away."

"If she marries Charles Rossitur it will be the ruin of him!" said Miss Masham. "What would become of him with such a wife?"

"He would evidently like to try the experiment, if all we hear be true," said the doctor; "and now, ladies, I am going to leave you to talk together while I go over and see how poor Sir John is to-day."

By special request of his host, Otway spent two whole days at the Chase, and as long as he was in the house both he and Letty were thoroughly uncomfortable. He treated her with the greatest coolness and indifference, although he was always courteous and polite; but whereas, in the past, he had been wont to ask her opinion, and to uphold it when given in defiance of every principle of reason and logic, he now calmly ignored her, and seemed to take every possible opportunity of showing how little worthy of notice were her remarks.

Neither did he fetch and carry for her as of old, and she might leave the room and return to it half-a-dozen times, and yet her movements never seemed to attract his attention.

And another trick he had that was particularly exasperating to her.   He would survey her with cold, critical eyes, and once he actually expressed disapproval of the way she wore her hair, and suggested an alteration. But Letty did not adopt the suggestion until he had left the Chase.

On his part he noticed that she avoided being alone with him ; unsuspected by her he made more than one attempt to secure a *tête-à-tête*, but she always baffled him.   He was not very clear as to his object in getting her to himself, but still he was deeply wounded by her evident determination to keep aloof from him.   Merely by accident on the day he was to leave they were alone together for ten minutes.   For a little while they spoke quite amiably of the beauty of the weather, and then he said— "I should like very much, if it were agreeable to you all, to come down for a few days to make the acquaintance of your sister-in-law when she arrives. You know she is a connexion of mine by marriage."

"I am sure papa will be very glad to see you," Letty answered. "Shall I tell him?"

"If you will be so kind."

"I thought perhaps—is it not likely?"— Letty began—"I mean are you not thinking of going back to America soon?"

"Certainly not," he answered, promptly. "Why should I?"

"But you might—I thought it possible— you know that—I mean—if you would like to marry someone out there——" She blurted out the last words in an awkward and shamefaced manner.

Otway burst out laughing. Letty thought it was such an unkind and unfeeling laugh. "Oh! I see," he said; "but I assure you I find that to be married once is quite as much happiness as I can bear; but if you would like to enter into that delightful contract a second time, pray do not let me stand in your way."

"You may be quite sure I shall consult my own convenience in every way," she answered.

"Without troubling yourself about me," he put in. "You meant that, I know, although you were too polite to say it. It is precisely what I should do myself, and it is quite as well that we should understand one another."

Glancing at her half-averted face, he saw by the scarlet cheeks and quivering lips that she was hurt or angry, or both. "Poor little woman," he said, half-aloud.

She turned upon him like a little fury. "How dare you pity me!" she cried. "Can you not understand that, although I might wish to free *you* from an obnoxious tie, it is a matter of perfect indifference to me what you do with your freedom? I am perfectly happy and contented, and all I ask is to be let alone."

"And a wish so reasonable deserves the utmost consideration!" he answered. "Allow me to apologise for having intruded upon you, and to say good-bye. I am going just now."

She stooped suddenly; took her dog, Orion, in her arms, and held his face to her own. "Oh, good-bye!" she said. "We will let you know when Mrs. John comes."

"Thank you," he answered. "Good-bye, Orion," and, before she could draw back, he bent down and kissed the little smooth head of the petted animal; but, whether by accident or design, his lips brushed Letty's fingers as well.

CHAPTER XIII.

THE FARMER'S SON.

It seems almost needless to explain that the doubts raised in Rossitur's mind of Lady Judith's fidelity by her own words were short-lived; she was right, in every way, he argued, to let the blame of their recent meetings rest upon him. That they were over was what was hard to bear, and it seemed to the poor fellow that now there was no hope left. It was impossible for him to struggle against the great odds opposed to him, and Lady Judith would also have to give way before the pressure that would be brought to bear upon her. On every side he was powerless. Handicapped by what they

called his plebeian birth, by his want of
money, and the probability—or rather, the
certainty—that if he ever became rich and
prosperous, he would no longer possess his
present advantages of youth and good looks,
what could he do? In a less prosaic age a
man could carry off the woman he loved, and
marry her before her friends could interfere ;
but such a feat was impossible when a net-
work of electric wires intersected the land!
And loyal lover though he was, there was still
deep down in Rossitur's heart the germ of a
doubt, if the doubt itself did not actually
exist, that Lady Judith, much as she loved
him, would not do anything desperate for his
sake. He was a million times more romantic
than she.

But surely there must be some road out of
the dilemma, the poor fellow thought to himself. He could not sit passive and see her
married to his rival without making some
effort to secure the happiness that seemed

more and more alluring as it was slipping from his grasp.

A few days after his stolen meetings with Lady Judith were discovered, he heard from his sister that Mr. Milbanke had come back from America, and was expected at Stilling-fort early the following week. The knowledge that he was so near, and that the marriage would now be hastened on, put the finishing stroke to the young man's despondency, and it was with a feeling half of fear and half of relief that Alice saw him making preparations for a journey. But he was only going to London, he said, for a few days. He had shown his ignorance of the world once in proposing to Lord Stillingfort for his daughter, and he was now bent upon a much more unconventional and absurd proceeding.

In the library of a handsome house in Grosvenor Square, John Milbanke, the future husband of the beautiful Lady Judith Forster, was seated, writing busily, a few days after his return from New York. He was a man of about fifty, and he looked his age; his hair was turning grey on the temples, there were a few crow's feet about his eyes; and the same eyes, although by no means as handsome, or as fully endowed with the power of passionate and pathetic language as those of his rival Charles Rossitur, were very sweet and kindly in expression, and gave a decided softness and charm to an otherwise somewhat stern face.

In figure he was tall and thin, but not ungainly; he was always well and carefully dressed, and he could no more have ventured to appear in the picturesque garments that so well became the handsome young musician of Stillingfort, than he could venture to attempt to fly through the air from London to Stone-shire. His voice, in speaking, was strong and melodious, and something in the clasp of his strong firm hand gave confidence in his sincerity and warmth of heart. Apart from his great wealth there was much in the man that was attractive in many respects, but he had a shrewd suspicion that but for his money Lady Judith would not have accepted his hand. This thought gave him intense pain when he allowed himself to dwell upon it, for she had inspired him with the first great passion of his life.

His first marriage had been one of convenience solely, and he had lived a lonely, conventional life; but now that middle age was past, and that by his wealth he could make life attractive and luxurious to the woman he loved, he longed to take to himself this girl whose beauty was more adorable in his eyes than the gold for which he had toiled so long.

He had before him now a letter from her father urging his immediate presence at Stillingfort; he was not disquieted by anything this epistle contained, and yet it left on his mind an impression that in his case, the proverbial delay would be dangerous indeed. With it had come a gay, prettily-worded, little *billet* from Judith herself. He had read it a dozen times at least without being able to make out whether the writer was jesting or in earnest, and he was in the act of laying down his pen in order to try once more, when a servant came in and presented a card.

"What is it, Campbell?" he said. "I am very busy this morning."

"A gentleman wishes to see you on business, sir. He says you do not know his name."

"Stay — what is it? Rossitur — never heard of him. Show him in;" and in a few moments he had risen to greet courteously his unknown visitor.

"Pray sit down, Mr. Rossitur," he said, in his kindly, affable way. "I have not the pleasure of knowing your name, but if I can do anything for you——"

Rossitur looked at him curiously, and the result of his investigation was not satisfactory. This man was not a mere agglomeration of money bags; the woman who had chosen him need not be ashamed of her choice, and not even when he stood pleading with Judith's father did his cause seem as hopeless as now that he was face to face with the man she had promised to marry! He laughed to himself as he mentally contrasted the homely room in his father's house at Stillingfort in which his work was done—the only spot on earth he could call his own—with this exquisitely-fitted and furnished chamber! And what was he to say now that he was here? Where were all the fine words wherewith he had meant to convince this man that he had no right to come between him and his love? Apparently, there was not one of them left upon his tongue.

He was not really many minutes silent while these thoughts were passing through

his mind ; and while Milbanke waited for his
unknown visitor to speak he watched him
curiously.   How handsome he was, and how
young ! And how gladly the middle-aged
millionaire would have given some thousands
if, by the sacrifice, he . could have gained
even a little of the grace and vigour of that
supple and nobly-proportioned form !

Rossitur at length raised his eyes and
spoke. " Before I came here," he said, " I
thought you could do a great deal for me ;
now I do not think you can help me at
all, or rather, I do not think you will help
me."

" I am sorry to hear I look so implacable,
or so ungenerous, or disagreeable."   Mr.
Milbanke began to think that his handsome
visitor was a little eccentric, to say the least
of it. " As I said before, I have not the
pleasure of knowing you, but if I can help
you it will give me pleasure to do so.   Pray
command me."

Rossitur laughed. " I am obliged to you,"
he said—then, after a pause, he added,
"Perhaps the best introduction I can give
is to tell you that I live at Stillingfort."
Milbanke's surprise showed on his face. " I
am the son of a tenant farmer on Lord
Stillingfort's estate, and I am organist of
the parish church." Then came a longer
pause. "I am a farmer's son," Rossitur
repeated, "and an organist ; and I have been
mad enough to fall in love with Lady Judith
Forster, his lordship's only daughter. Now,
Mr. Milbanke, do you know what I have
come to you for ?"

Milbanke, with his elbow on the writing-
table, was biting the end of his long quill
pen ; his eyes were on the letter he had been
writing. " That is not so very strange, is it ?
That you have fallen in love with her, I
mean," he said. He began to think that his
visitor was not merely eccentric, but mad.

" Then you do not blame me ?" the young

man cried. "You do not think I am presumptuous?"

" Pardon me—I did not say so."

" I am told," Rossitur went on, "that you
want to marry her, and what chance have I
against your riches? I can give her nothing
but love; but I thought if you were but
generous and unselfish you would not stand
in the way of our happiness. Is it too much
to ask, sir? Are we poor men to have
nothing because we are too poor to buy?
She would marry me—I know she would
if you would give her up."

The words grated sorely on Milbanke's
ears. Was it possible that the girl he loved
favoured this man—that he was in truth her
accepted lover? But no; she was too proud
to listen to such as he, and this wild talk
meant nothing; it would be absurd to pay
any heed to it. He must just humour the
poor fellow, and get rid of him as soon as
possible.

"Mr. Rossitur," he said, "I am sure you will believe me when I tell you that, if I thought you had any reason for supposing that Lady Judith Forster was attached to you and anxious to become your wife, I should at once resign my claim to her hand; but, and I beg of you to excuse me for speaking plainly, I think you have deluded yourself. She has consented of her own free will to become my wife, and until she releases me I do not mean to give her up to any man."

"You do not then suppose it possible for her to be persuaded into this marriage with you because you are rich? You believe she accepts you of her own free will?"

Milbanke smiled. "You are very pertinacious, sir, and not very complimentary to me. Now, you must excuse me if I put this question beyond all doubt by allowing you to read a passage in a letter received by me from Lady Judith Forster this morning. I

have only fully understood it myself since
you honoured me with this visit."

Rossitur took the letter. "You wish me
to read this?" he said.

"Certainly; the passage I have marked by
folding down."

And he read it through with Milbanke's
eyes fixed upon his face; but the meaning of
the words did not all at once come home
to him. The writer, in a sort of fable, re-
lated how, like the heroine of a novel, she
was beset by the attentions of a handsome
rustic, who had actually been mad enough
to propose marriage to her through her
father. She described how he waylaid her
in her walks and told all his friends that
if she were a free agent she would choose
him for her husband; she also playfully
cautioned Milbanke against the jealous rage
of this disappointed swain, and concluded by
saying "the poor fellow is very handsome,
certainly, but he is not a gentleman, and

of course, I never gave him any encourage-
ment."

It would be impossible to give any
adequate idea of Rossitur's feelings as he
read this letter through. It stamped him at
once in his own eyes as the easy dupe of
a heartless woman's vanity and caprice, and
her object in writing it was as patent to him
as his own despised and insulted love. She
wanted to make herself safe in case any
rumour of her intercourse with the "rustic
lover" should reach Milbanke's ears. Against
such double dealing he was powerless; the
only letter he had ever received from her was
destroyed by her desire—he kept it as long as
he dared—so there was nothing left for him
but to throw up his cards and acknowledge
himself beaten! She had fooled him all
round ; and to reiterate that, if he had been
presumptuous, she had led him on, would
but confirm the assertion made in her letter.

He gave it back to Milbanke, and after a

struggle of a few seconds to gain command over his voice, he said, "I am not, it is true, a gentleman by birth, but I hope I have the instincts of one. You meant to silence me, and to teach me a lesson, by giving me that letter to read, and you have done both most effectually. I can but apologise for my intrusion, but before I go, grant me one favour. Do not humiliate me further in my own eyes by speaking of my visit to—to her."

"You may depend upon me," Milbanke answered. Then, as if struck by a sudden thought, be rose hurriedly, and, laying his hand on Rossitur's shoulder, said in a low constrained voice, "I am not quite satisfied, sir, and Lady Judith's happiness is very dear to me. Tell me, as between man and man, have you been under a delusion in this matter or have you not ?"

"I have been under a most complete delusion, except as regards my own feelings," Rossitur answered, "but I am fully per-

suaded that Lady Judith's happiness will be
secured by her marriage with you ; she has
explained, in a manner not to be mistaken,
what she thinks of my pretensions, and there
is no more to be said."

When his visitor was gone, Milbanke sat
and pondered long. "I must keep my
word," he said at last, "and not mention
this visit to her ; but I should like to tell
her that she is mistaken about her 'rustic
lover.' He is a gentleman."

CHAPTER XIV.

WHEN Herbert Otway went back to London
after his short visit, a blank and sad interval
of waiting for news set in at the Chase.
Having brooded exclusively on his loss for
a week or more, Sir John naturally began to
fix his thoughts upon his grandson and the
young widow, and to plan for their reception
at their future home. A certain suite of
rooms must be refurnished for "poor, dear
Amy," and within easy reach of them were
the long unused nurseries in which poor
Jack and Letty had played as children.

Someone suggested that Mrs. Erskine
would probably bring a native nurse over
with her, but Sir John declared that he

would not have the "creature" at the Chase.
"My grandson must have a respectable
Englishwoman, not a heathen, to look after
him," he said.

Miss Lambton, in her quiet way, wondered
whether Rossitur, the maid, would come with
her mistress to England, or remain in India
with her husband. Nothing was known at
the Chase about Pottinger at that time.

"Poor Jack said in one of his letters, I
remember," Letty remarked, "that when he
came home, Pottinger should come with him,
as he was so clever about horses. Why
should not Amy keep Rossitur, as she likes
her so much?—and Pottinger might leave
the regiment and be our extra groom. We
must have a couple more men in the stables
if papa gives Amy a carriage and horses of
her own."

"I think, dear," said Aunt Louise, "it will
be better to give up the barouche and the
greys to Amy, and to let me have a little

basket affair, with a quiet pony that I can drive myself."

"Well, well," cried Sir John, "we can settle it all when Mrs. John comes. Perhaps she ought to have the barouche and the greys; but I am not at all sure that I want that woman Rossitur here. I do not much like what I know of her or her people. Her father has lived the life of a hermit since his wife left him years ago. He is a capital farmer and all that, Murray tells me, but no one ever sees him; and then there is that son of his—a musical genius, I am told—who set his cap at Judith Forster; but she is engaged to Milbanke, the millionaire. I do not fancy, myself, having any of the Rossitur lot here; but if we must, we must, I suppose."

As the days of expectation before the arrival of the Indian mail went by, Letty got very weary of conversations such as the above. It was a matter of indifference to

her whether the widow brought a nurse with
her or not, or whether the famous Rossitur
continued to act as Amy's maid or remained
in India.   She was prepared to welcome and
love her sister-in-law for Jack's sake, and it
would be a sad pleasure to have his baby
boy; but, of course, Amy's presence in the
house would make a great difference, and it
was impossible to tell how she would get on
with them and they with her.   She might be
a very agreeable inmate and a pleasant
addition to their small circle, and she might
be the very reverse; but such as she was she
must be endured and made the best of;
there was no possibility of escape.

As Letty made this rather querulous remark
to herself it flashed across her that there was
an alternative open to her; that if the Chase
became an unhappy, instead of a happy home,
she had but to humble herself to the man who
was her husband, and he would let her have
her proper place in his home.   Humble her-

self! The word and all that it implied made
her hot all over. Stoop to ask the man who
told her he was learning to despise her, to
assert his rights and give her protection even
if love were impossible! Never! She knew
she had acted like a vain, heartless, silly child,
and put herself beyond the pale of his forgiveness, and that if she could but blot out
the few hours that immediately succeeded
the marriage ceremony, not only from her
memory but out of the history of her life, she
might now be the happiest of women instead
of the most miserable.

But effacement was impossible; and, indeed, it seemed as if every day her remem-
brance of all she had said and done during
the drive to Richmond, and after, grew
sharper and clearer every day. No wonder
he was changed; treatment less odious and
unwomanly might well have turned a man's
love to gall. But how amply he was avenged
had he but known it! She had wilfully

blinded herself as long as she could, but
even before their late unsatisfactory and
most awkward meeting, she knew it was only
by lashing her pride into activity, by recall-
ing the words, " I despise you," that she was
able to keep the love she now felt for him
within reasonable bounds.

At last the long expected Indian letter
arrived ; it was the short epistle written,
as the reader knows, by Rossitur for her
mistress, to catch the mail that left the day
but one after poor Jack Erskine's death.
Sir John was very much pleased with it,
short though it was, and he read it to his
friend, Dr. Murray, with tears in his eyes.

" The poor dear girl is quite broken-
hearted ; anyone can see that," he said.

A much longer letter arrived the following week. Lying on a couch, dressed in a
loose white tea-gown, with her beautiful hair
streaming about her, and Victor de Louvain's
lately received, kind letter of condolence

serving as a marker in the half-read novel
that lay near her hand, Amy Erskine had
dictated that letter to Rossitur, and Rossitur
wrote it fluently.   That she did not adhere
strictly to the dictated words was a matter
of no moment, for her power of expressing
thoughts in language far exceeded that of her
mistress, and Amy never asked to see the
letters when they were finished.

This particular letter of course contained
details of the accident.   " My poor darling"
—this was what they read at the Chase, and
the father, aunt and sister got lumps in their
throats as one read aloud and the others
listened ; they were so pleased, although
so pained, to hear everything that had
been said and done by " poor dear Jack,"
just before he died — "my poor darling came
back to luncheon with three or four men that
dreadful, DREADFUL day,"—Rossitur put
the second " dreadful" in capital letters her
mistress laid such emphasis on it—" and

he was in such good spirits, and looked so
bright and handsome."—"And how you and
he wrangled," thought Rossitur—" We had
such a merry luncheon, and he scolded me,
in fun, you know, because I would not go
to the polo ground.   Just think how awful it
would have been if I had been there !   It
would have killed me to see him fall !   I
know it would.   It was poor Pottinger who
brought home the news ; but a friend of
mine who happened to be here stopped
him before he saw me, for, unfortunately, the
poor faithful fellow was quite out of his mind !
It was all most terrible !   First to see my
precious Jack brought home to me dead, and
to know that I had lost him, and that our
darling boy was an orphan !   Then poor
Pottinger—he is the husband, you know,
of my faithful Rossitur—he went quite mad
that night, and they took him away next day,
and by this, I believe, he is on his way to
England to be put into a lunatic asylum.

I do hope the poor dear fellow will get
all right again.   My excellent Rossitur and
her little boy—he is just a month older than
my *one solace*—are with me here, of course ;
and as soon as I hear from you, dear Sir
John, I shall make my plans.   In your kind
telegram you say ' come home at once,' and
it is my most fervent desire to get to England
quickly, and to put darling Jack's boy into
your arms ; but I do not feel equal to the
long, lonely journey just yet ; and I very
much dread an English winter.   Is Stoneshire very cold ?   I think sometimes I should
like ·on my arrival to go to the South of
France, or to Sorrento, near Naples—I have
long desired to see Italy — live quietly
through the long, sad winter and then go
to the dear Chase — my darling so often
described his beautiful home to me — in
spring, when the east winds are over.   This
plan may not meet with your approval, but of
course I should like as much as possible

to be guided by you. I know what my precious husband would say if he were alive. He would say, "*By all means, my darling, winter at Sorrento,*" but I feel that you, being his father, have a sort of right to dictate to me what I am to do, and where I am to go. I shall, however, manage to see something of Italy on my way home, as I may never have another opportunity."

"Poor darling! Poor child! How feelingly she writes!" said Sir John, as he wiped his eyes. She really bears up wonderfully; but, of course, she knows it is her duty for the sake of my grandson. And that poor man, Pottinger, out of his mind! Dear me! Dear me! That is very shocking. And poor Amy will be hampered with his child as well as her own until she gets to England."

"She seems quite as devoted to Rossitur as ever," said Letty.

"And what do you think of her project of wintering in France or Italy?" asked Miss

Lambton. "I am sure Stoneshire ought to be warm enough for anyone."

"Oh, it is preposterous!" cried Sir John. "I cannot allow it. If she feels the cold she must buy a lot of furs and wrap up warm. I do not want the child to be taken to any of those ill-drained, smelly places. I must write at once and tell her I cannot allow it. She says she will be guided by me."

"I hope she will," Letty said to herself. She was not as favourably impressed by the tone of her sister-in-law's letter as Sir John, and she was angry with herself for being so critical.

It so happened, however, that something occurred in connection with the letter which made her dislike it even more than she did at first.

CHAPTER XV.

LOVE AND PRIDE.

" I WISH papa had not asked me to send it," Letty said to herself. " He ought to remember how awkward it is for me to write to him ! I do not know what to say, and I must say something. I cannot put it in an envelope and send it without a word, and if I make a fuss about it papa will be angry."

The "it" in question was Mrs. John Erskine's letter, which Sir John had desired his daughter to send on to Otway to read, with a request that he would return it.

" She is a kind of relation of his, you know," Sir John said, "and it will interest him to hear all about my poor boy's death ; and I want to know what he has to say about

Amy's plan—you can tell him I totally dis-
approve of it—of wintering abroad. As if
we hadn't as fine a climate as any in the
world. I am quite sure winter never lasts
more than six or seven months in Stoneshire, and it is generally fine, open weather,
when the scent lies and a man comes home
well-splashed after his day's hunting. And if
there is any hard frost look at our skating.
What is there in those stinking foreign places
to make up for our hunting and skating?
You send on that letter at once, Letty, and
let me hear what Otway has to say."

And Letty took the letter without demur.
It was not until she sat down to carry
out her father's wishes that she found how
difficult it was to perform a very simple task.

"DEAR MR. OTWAY," she began, "papa
wishes you to read the enclosed letter from
Amy—my sister-in-law. It came by last
mail. You will see all she says about poor
dear Jack. I wish she had told us a little

more. Please return the letter, but there is no hurry about it. Papa wants to know what you think of Amy's plan of wintering abroad ; he does not like the idea at all, and wishes her to come home at once.

"Believe me——"

She got so far and stopped short; how should she wind up her note, and how sign herself? She was not Letty Erskine, and she could not bring herself to put Letty Otway; "Letty" without any surname was too friendly and familiar; and, besides, that was the way she had always signed her letters during her engagement. Many and many time had she written "Always your own Letty," or "Your most affectionate Letty!"

Was it possible that she had ever thus subscribed herself to him? And what madness had come over her on that most wretched day? It must have been madness. No sane woman could have behaved as she

had done.   And in her misconception of
Otway's character how utterly wrong she had
been in her forecast of his action in the affair.
She had imagined herself yielding slowly to
his prayers and entreaties, and growing more
and more tolerant of his never ending
adulation of her many perfections.   And lo!
she had wounded him with a blow so sharp
and cruel that he had turned upon her and
proved that the ardent, devoted lover was a
man with a will as strong and pride as unbending as her own.

"'Believe me——' What *am* I to say? I
know what *he* believes me to be—a heartless, unwomanly little wretch, who played
with him for her own amusement; stole his
love, and then flung it in his face. *That* is
what he believes me to be.   If I were to
write, 'Believe me to be your own, loving,
sorry, ashamed, repentant and broken-hearted
wife,' it would be the truth."   She wrote the
words as fast as her pen could move, at the

end of the note and then looked at them
with tears blinding her eyes.

"Now I have spoiled that and I must
write another," she said, presently. "What
a goose I am!" She took a second sheet,
copied out what she had already written,
and again stopped short at the "Believe
me." "I am just as much puzzled as before!"
she said, and thrusting both the notes out of
sight into the leaves of her blotting-book,
she took a third sheet and wrote as follows
without any formal beginning or end—"Papa
wishes me to send you the enclosed, which
please return when you have quite done with
it. It is from my sister-in-law. Papa wants
to know what you think of her plan of
wintering abroad. He does not approve of
it."

"There; that will do capitally!" she said,
as she finished. "Why did I not think of
that before? What have I done with the
other stupid notes? I must take care not

to put one of them—*the* one, up in mistake.
I think I got out of my difficulty very
cleverly. I wonder if he will send an
answer, and how he will sign himself?"

On the second morning the answer came;
and Letty's cheeks tingled with mortification
and disappointment, and a little anger as
well, as she read—"Mr. Herbert Otway
presents his compliments to Mrs. Herbert
Otway, and begs that she will thank Sir
John for so kindly sending him Mrs. John
Erskine's letter. It is herewith returned.
Mr. Otway does not see anything to object
to in Mrs. John Erskine's desire to winter
abroad."

"Mr. Otway sees nothing against Amy's
plan of wintering abroad, papa, and he is
very much obliged to you for letting him see
her letter."

"He sees nothing against it? Well, *I* see
everything; you had a letter from Otway,
then—what does he say?"

" Nothing but what I told you just now ;
he wrote just a few lines."

" I thought he had too much sense to
advocate that ridiculous fad of wintering at
Sorrento ; but I have written to tell her what
I think, and I expect that she will be guided
by me and come home at once. I must
really stir them up about her rooms or they
will not be ready in time."

It had given Otway quite as much trouble
to frame a reply to Letty as it had given
Letty in the first place to write to him. It•
is unfortunate in some cases that we have
no better grounds for the formation of our
judgments than what is actually before us.
Otway had no possible means of knowing
that Letty had spent more than an hour
trying to write what she considered a
proper letter to him before she concocted
the business-like epistle, which might have
been addressed to a tradesman with an
order for some goods ; and when she read

his business-like reply it never occurred to
her that he had dashed off a much more
elaborate letter, wherein, when he had com-
mented briefly upon Mrs. John Erskine's
Indian budget, he gave the news of the day
in a light and agreeable fashion. Otway
had a facile pen, and it pleased him to use
it for Letty's benefit.

Yet as soon as the letter was finished he
tore it up in such a determined manner that
it seemed as if he were venting a fit of anger
upon the unoffending paper.

" She will probably look upon it as an
impertinence if I write to her in that way,"
he said ; and then he wrote the formal note
in the third person which caused poor Letty
such bitter disappointment.

He was engaged that very day to dine
at Richmond with his old acquaintances,
Mrs. Ogilvey and her husband ; it was to be
a farewell party, made up of the people he
was accustomed to meet at Queen's Gate

Terrace, and before he got back to town
he would be called upon to decide whether to
go with the Ogilveys in their yacht for a
cruise to Norway or by himself to the Black
Forest.

Mr. Ogilvey had taken a great fancy to
him ; and, although Otway was not specially
drawn to him, or prepared to look upon him
as an intimate friend, he could not, without
positive rudeness, refuse the hospitality so
perpetually offered to him ; and, by degrees,
he found that he spent more time with
him and his wife than he did with other and
older friends.

Mrs. Ogilvey never alluded to the secret
she had entrusted to him when her acquaintance with him was renewed in the early days
of his engagement to Letty Erskine, and the
affair was, of course, sacred to him. He was
glad to see that there was apparently perfect
accord between the husband and wife, and
when, after the manner of women, Mrs.

Ogilvey found out all about his sudden separation from his bride, he could not refuse the sympathy so abundantly lavished upon him. But it was never agreeable to him to hear Letty blamed, yet, as he had assumed the *rôle* of the outraged and unforgiving one, he could not consistently break out in her defence.

Mrs. Ogilvey went very cautiously and subtly to work to try and persuade him — always for Letty's sake — to have the marriage declared null and void ; and sorely against his wish Otway, as he replied to her arguments, was obliged to admit that, sooner or later, the only way out of a difficulty not created by him would be to set his wife legally free.

Mrs. Ogilvey had no clearly defined object in wishing to bring about this separation, but nevertheless, she wished it with all her heart. She could not marry Otway herself, and there was no one to whom she was anxious to see him married, but she fancied that he would be more absolutely her friend if the tie that bound him to Letty was broken, and she could not endure the thought that he was still attached to her.

Her chance of success would have been even less than it was could he have had even a passing glimpse of one of the letters Letty had hidden away in her blotting-book. What a revelation and revolution there would have been could he have read the words "your own loving, sorry, ashamed, repentant and broken-hearted wife, Letty," if only she had—as so often happens in books, and so rarely in real life—slipped the wrong letter into the envelope, and so have let it reach him unawares. By the very next train he would have started for Little Centre Bridge, and, without waiting for the useless formality of an explanation, have clasped the repentant girl in his arms and sealed their reconciliation with a hundred kisses.

But, all unknown to him, the letter that would have worked such wonders lay between the leaves of the blotter, and Letty herself forgot that she had not destroyed it.

Otway was in the act of dressing for the Richmond dinner when a telegram was put into his hand. It was from Mrs. Ogilvey, and contained bad news—" My husband is taken suddenly and dangerously ill. Come at once. He has asked for you."

Before the end of the week Otway was standing beside Mr. Ogilvey's grave in Kensal Green, and under the dead man's will he was appointed one of the executors, and trustee also for the widow, to whom, under certain conditions, the husband had left the whole of his immense wealth.

CHAPTER XVI.

THE MEETING IN THE PORCH.

CHARLES ROSSITUR went back to Stillingfort an altered man. Disappointed love, the impotent rage of jealousy and shame at his own weakness, were fighting a pitched battle within him, and these foes of equal power had no chance, the one against the other. But as the contest waxed and waned, love first gave way. It stung the poor young fellow to the quick to know that the woman he worshipped had simply stooped for a while to his level merely to mock him. That with his kisses warm upon her lips she could calmly hold him up to the ridicule of the man she meant to marry !

It was only by degrees that the utter baseness of her conduct came home to him. How certain she was that Milbanke would take her explanation as the true one should any hint of her intimacy with the organist come to his ears; and if she had known that Rossitur contemplated the folly of a visit to his rival she could not have laid her plans more craftily to checkmate him.

To tell the truth, Lady Judith was driven to her last refuge when Lord Stillingfort suddenly appeared before her and Rossitur in Warleigh Copse, and took her away without allowing her even one word of farewell; she knew then that she must make her choice between love and Mammon, and abide by it. As a matter of fact she had already chosen, but she wanted to keep her handsome, romantic lover with her as long as possible, unmindful of the anguish he might suffer when at last it dawned upon him that she did not mean to throw Milbanke over.

Her father put the risk she was running

before her in very plain language. " If you loved this low-born fellow well enough to marry him, I could find it in my heart to forgive you," he said, " but you know you do not. You admire his handsome face— you like to show your power over him, but if I were to say to you now, ' Marry him,' you would not do it." And then he made her give him a solemn promise, from that moment, to hold no more intercourse with him.

And she gave the promise with the intention of keeping it, but she could not understand why Rossitur himself made no attempt to see her. She had neither heard from him nor seen him, even by accident, from the moment she left him standing alone in Warleigh Copse ; he was at home, she knew, for amongst a hundred players she could recognise his touch upon the organ at morning service, and never had the exquisite aria, " He shall feed his flock,"

played by him as the congregation left the
church on the Sunday after their last meeting,
thrilled and saddened her as it did that day.
Was it because he had taught it to her,
and many and many a time played it to
her himself in those never-to-be-forgotten
first days of their acquaintance ?

He was never happy now, poor fellow,
unless when seated at the organ. With his
fingers on the keys he felt the equal of the
best blood in England ; and yet his beloved
art had lost much of its power to calm and
heal the perturbed and sorely bruised spirit
within him, and his sister Alice, and one
other—a woman also—watched him with sad
and anxious eyes.

Milbanke arrived at the Park some two
or three days after his strange interview
with Rossitur ; he and Lady Judith were
to be seen together constantly, and it was
rumoured that he was pressing for an early
marriage. All her uneasiness had vanished ;

Milbanke was the most generous and devoted of lovers ; and if she sometimes gave a sigh of regret in secret for the man who in all save birth and wealth, was an ideal husband, no one could have imagined from her manner to her future possessor that there was a thought of her heart unshared by him.

The news had come to Stillingfort of the sad tragedy at Simla. Bella Rossitur, or Mrs. Pottinger, as she was naturally called in her native village, wrote a detailed account of Captain Erskine's death, and described the sudden insanity of her own husband, with the zest of one to whom the narration of disagreeable news is more or less a pleasant occupation.

" Bella was never troubled with much feeling," her brother observed, when Alice read the letter aloud to him. " Unfortunate George Pottinger might be a complete stranger to her instead of her husband and the father of her child, to judge by the way she writes of him. Poor old George! How bewitched he was about her!" and Rossitur sighed. But he often sighed now.

Presently he grew excited and angry as his sister went on reading the letter. " I have been expecting to hear great news about Charles and her young ladyship," Mrs. Pottinger wrote. " Does he still give her lessons on the organ, and what chance has he of marrying her?"

" How dare you gossip to Bella about me and Lady Judith?" Rossitur interrupted, sternly. " Do you not know that she has no respect for the feelings of anyone belonging to her, and that it would delight her mischievous spirit to hear that I had been disappointed and made a fool of? There! Do not read any more for me. Perhaps the next news she hears of her unhappy brother will startle her more than the news of his marriage to the earl's daughter would have done."

He went to the house door, which was always open in fine weather, and stood there looking out in the direction, of Stillingfort Woods. "How beautiful they are," he thought, "and what madly happy moments I have spent in them. And they will look as beautiful when she is married and I am —gone."

The sound of trotting horses along the high road that led past the farm caught his ears; he turned and saw a lady and gentleman approaching with two grooms in attendance. The lady was Lady Judith; the gentleman, Milbanke. They were going at a rapid pace, and now and then they exchanged a gay remark.

She looked well in the saddle, and sat her horse to perfection; he looked to less advantage, and Rossitur, who had ridden the roughest and wildest of horses from his boyhood, smiled, half with pity and half with derision, as he looked at his rival's ungainly seat and awkward grasp of the reins.

It was impossible for the riders to go past the house without noticing the young man, who was leaning in dejection against the door-post; but whether they saw him or not, there was no recognition. His eyes followed Lady Judith; the sight of her may have given him both pleasure and pain; it is impossible to say which he felt most keenly, for the smile raised by the horsemanship of her companion did not leave his lips.

About fifty yards from the house there was a gate which opened into a field, and over the gate there was a white-faced cow solemnly staring. Milbanke's horse caught sight of what seemed to him a horrible apparition, and swerving aside with a sudden jerk, for which the rider was wholly unprepared, it rose on its hind legs, and after a struggle to right itself, fell back, and lay kicking and plunging on the road.

With a loud scream for help Lady Judith sprang from her horse.   She had but recently heard of the death of young John Erskine by a fall from his pony at polo, and how terrible it would be if the tragedy of his sad death were to be repeated now.

Ere her trembling limbs could carry her to the spot where her companion was lying, the horse was on its legs again, and Charles Rossitur was on his knees beside the senseless Milbanke.   Not a word was spoken as he made a rapid examination, and before it was over, his sister and several of the farm servants came running up.

" Is he—is he dead?" Judith managed to gasp out at last ; and either unconsciously, or to give emphasis to her words, she laid her hand on Rossitur's shoulder.

He shivered as he felt the touch ! When last her hand was laid there he was allowed to clasp it in his own — to press it to his lips, and to gaze unchecked into the glorious

eyes that were now fixed in horror upon
Milbanke's pale and blood-stained face.

" You need not be alarmed, Lady Judith,"
Rossitur answered, quietly ; but he could not
wholly conquer the tremor in his voice. " He
is not dead ; not even seriously hurt, I hope.
He fell on a sharp stone, and the blood you
see is from the cut ; but I am afraid his leg
is broken just below the knee by a kick from
the horse as it was struggling to get up.
May I send one of your grooms for the
doctor ? And Alice," addressing his sister,
"get me some brandy."

But the stimulant restored only temporary
consciousness to the sufferer. At the first
attempt to move him he fainted again, and
then Rossitur declared that it would not be
safe to take him to the Park.

" Our house is quite at his service and at
yours, Lady Judith," he said, in answer to
her faint remonstrances, as he helped his
men to place Milbanke on the hurdles that

were brought. "It is only a poor place, as
you know, but we can make him comfortable."

She acquiesced in silence ; neither did
she make any remonstrance when Rossitur
despatched a man on horseback to counter-
mand the carriage that had already been
ordered from the Park.

Very quickly and quietly Milbanke was
conveyed to the farm, and then it seemed to
Lady Judith that everyone had forgotten her.
Left alone outside she wondered what she
ought to do. She could not make up her
mind to go away, and yet she seemed out
of place there ; for although no one had a
better right than she to be with Milbanke,
she had not the courage to take her place
beside him as long as he was under the roof
of, and befriended in his time of need by, the
man she had so cruelly wronged.

Half-an-hour passed, and still she waited ;
the doctor drove up in a hurry and disap-

peared into the house, and she began to feel at last so faint and weary that she went into the rose-covered porch, and, taking off her hat, she leaned against the wall and closed her eyes.

Was it really anxiety for her future husband that made her heart beat so loudly; that brought the colour alternately rushing to and fading from her cheeks, and kept her from going quietly home to wait there for the next news? As the minutes passed and no one came to her she felt oppressed and humiliated by the neglect, which was after all not unnatural under the circumstances. She grew calmer by degrees as she sat in the porch with her eyes closed. She forgot to wonder what was going on inside the house; forgot her desire for notice and attention of some kind, and lulled at last by the stillness she fell into a sort of doze.

And it was thus Rossitur found her when he came out to tell her that the broken leg was set, and the patient once more conscious, although he had not yet spoken. But she did not hear the step, and on seeing her seated there with closed eyes and the slightly-parted, rich red lips, the only sign of life as it were in her face, he stopped short, and for a few seconds the love he was striving with all his might to tear out of his heart overmastered him, and he involuntarily uttered her name aloud.

She started and looked at him, but her self-control was perfect. "Oh, Mr. Rossitur," she said, "how you frightened me. I am waiting here for some news. How is he? Is there any danger? I know you will tell me the truth."

He looked at her for a moment or two with a curious, steadfast gaze; then he said, very quietly, "I am glad nothing has happened to shake your trust in me, Lady Judith. You need not be anxious about Mr. Milbanke. He is not in the slightest danger as the simple fracture of his leg is his most dangerous hurt."

"Will you not shake hands and let me thank you?" she cried, impulsively, as she saw that he was about to leave her again alone. "Why should there be this estrangement? Mr. Milbanke will——"

She stopped suddenly, and her outstretched hand fell to her side. Rossitur had not taken it. "Pardon me, Lady Judith," he said, "but I desire no thanks from either you or Mr. Milbanke. I did no more for him than I should have done for any of our farm labourers in the same state. As to estrangement," and he gave a little laugh, "I do not know what you mean. I have simply fallen again into my proper place, and I do think I shall never touch your hand again."

He went past her through the porch as he spoke, and, turning round the angle of the house, he disappeared and she saw him no more.

CHAPTER XVII.

A TERRIBLE TEMPTATION.

"AND you refuse to accept any favour at my hands? I am very sorry—very much grieved and disappointed, I assure you."

The speaker was Mr. Milbanke, now quite recovered from the effects of his accident, and it was Charles Rossitur whom he addressed. It was Milbanke's last day at the farm; the carriage was expected every moment to take him to the Park, and he had sent for his young host in order to make him an offer which he had been considering in his own mind for some time past.

It was a handsome and liberal offer, but Rossitur refused it without a moment's hesitation.

Milbanke, who had recently purchased a princely estate and picturesque old house in Dashshire, and had built and endowed a handsome church to meet the urgent needs of a rapidly increasing neighbourhood, offered Rossitur the post of organist and choir-master, with a salary of three hundred a year and a furnished house rent free.

"It is one of the prettiest houses on the estate," Milbanke said, "and I could very easily have one of the rooms enlarged so as to take in a chamber - organ if you wish——"

"You are very kind — very generous," Rossitur had said, "but I cannot accept anything from you. A few shillings to the farm labourers who carried you here after the accident is quite enough; but if you feel heavily in our debt, and wish to discharge your obligation, send my sister a new-fashioned churn for her dairy—she is fond of new things — or our father that newly-

invented chaff-cutter he has set his heart
upon."

"I have already ordered it for him, and I
shall add the churn for your sister. Also,
pray take this note and divide it among the
men as you see fit." He gave Rossitur five
pounds as he spoke, and then added, "But it
is for yourself I wish to do something. Are
you so wedded to this place that you cannot
bear to leave it ?"

"By no means. I have made up my mind
to go away."

"May I ask where ?"

"That I cannot tell you, for I do not know
myself ; but it will be to some place a long
way off." There was a strange look in his
eyes as he spoke, but Milbanke did not
notice it.

"Then I suppose there is no more to be
said," he answered, "and I am very much
disappointed. I had set my heart upon
having you at my new church. You will

have everything your own way there, remember."

" Mr. Milbanke," Rossitur interrupted,
"why do you make this offer to me? You
have never alluded to—and I am grateful to
you for ignoring, my folly—our interview at
your house in town; but at the same time
you cannot have forgotten what I told you
then."

" Why allude to it now?" Milbanke
answered, with a touch of impatience in
his tone. " Foolish things are better forgotten, are they not?"

" Yes; but you must remember that I told
you I loved the lady you are about to marry;
and why you should go out of your way
to throw me into hers, is what I cannot
understand."

Milbanke's colour perceptibly rose. " I
do it," he said, " because I wish to prove
to you how little importance I attach to your
confession for love to Lady Judith Forster.

There is nothing between you and her, and there never has been anything. That you admired her and that she noticed your admiration is natural enough ; but what of that ?"

Rossitur was silent. It was perfectly evident that Lady Judith had successfully thrown dust in Milbanke's eyes, and the man she had first befooled was too generous to betray her. " She has played her cards well," he said rather bitterly to himself, "and it is a pity she should not enjoy her winnings. If I were malicious I could snatch them all from her ; but she seems to know pretty well that she is safe. She has not even asked me not to betray her ; but perhaps it is best." And yet, in spite of his philosophy, his companion's words, " but what of that ?" were not pleasant to hear.

He saw that Milbanke was expecting an answer of some kind, so at last he spoke. " It was very absurd on my part, sir," he said, "to expect you to look with anything but ridicule at my folly and presumption. I had no right to raise my eyes to Lady Judith Forster; but I hold the cure of my folly in my own hands, and perhaps I shall use it— who knows? Now, allow me to thank you once more and, believe me, I do so most sincerely, for the offer you have made me, and I am sorry that I cannot accept it. Here is the carriage; let me give you my arm."

"If you think better of it by and by, you have only to let me know," were Milbanke's last words as he drove off. He was thankful for his recovery, and for release from his confinement; satisfied with himself, also, for his generosity to the "farmer's son," and radiant with delight at the thought that in a week from that day Lady Judith would be his wife.

"How admirably she must have behaved," he said to himself, as the carriage that was taking him back to her turned in at the Park gates. "And how difficult it must have been to show that very touchy young man how presumptuous he was to aspire to her, without hurting his feelings. But Judith has good sense and admirable tact."

That same evening one of Lord Stillingfort's footmen delivered a note at the farm. It was addressed in Lady Judith's writing to "C. Rossitur, Junior." Time was when to get a note from her made his heart leap for joy. Now he took it and opened it quietly enough. It was very short. "DEAR MR. ROSSITUR," it ran, "Can you come over early to-morrow, say twelve o'clock? I want to see you on business. Please ask for me. Sincerely yours, J. F."

Punctually at twelve the following day he was shown into a pretty morning-room, and he found there, apparently waiting for him, Lady Judith and Mr. Milbanke. "What does all this mean?" he thought to himself; but he fancied he knew.

Milbanke rose and shook hands with him ; Lady Judith bowed and kept her seat. She looked a little nervous, and her colour kept coming and going as it always did when she was excited. Rossitur was not excited in the least ; indeed, he felt as if he were looking on at a performance in which he had no part.

Mr. Milbanke leaned over the young lady and said something in a whisper. A look of relief came into her face as she answered aloud, " Very well. I think you are right," and raising her hand with old - fashioned courtesy to his lips, he left the room.

The door had barely closed behind him when Lady Judith rose hurriedly and went towards Rossitur, holding out her hand. " You will not refuse it to-day ?" she said, almost humbly, and he took it.

She kept it in her own, and looked at him with an appealing half-frightened glance. She was visibly agitated now ; her breathing was rapid, her colour shifted almost every moment, and the fingers that had closed round Rossitur's were as cold as ice. " How can I thank you enough for coming?" she said. " I have so much to say to you—will you not sit down?"

He drew his hand away, and said in such a cold, matter-of-fact tone, " With pleasure, Lady Judith. I am quite at your service," that the expression of her face changed in a moment and she gave a little shiver.

" I·hardly know how to begin," she said, as she nervously played with the lace trimming of her dress. " If we were in the habit of meeting every day it would be different; but you see—you understand——"

" I understand perfectly, Lady Judith, that when your father put a stop to our meetings in the wood I had no chance of meeting you anywhere. If I were a young gentleman, and belonged to the county set, we might have many opportunities of seeing one another at dinner and tennis parties and balls, but as I am only a poor organist and the son of a farmer, I have had no chance. My own feeling now is that it would have been better —for me, at least—if we had never met."

" Oh, do not say so !" she exclaimed, fixing her beautiful eyes upon him. " You know— you must know that if—if I could have chosen for myself——"

" You would have been sensible enough to choose the rich man instead of the poor one. Why do you reproach yourself, Lady Judith? I do not reproach you ; and pardon me for reminding you, but you said you wanted to see me on business."

" You are very much changed since our last meeting," she broke in, with a touch of petulance in her tone.

" Our last meeting took place in the porch of my father's house," he said, "the day of Mr. Milbanke's accident, and I have not changed in any respect since that day".

" I do not call that our last meeting," she

retorted, quickly ; " but we will not waste time arguing. Mr. Milbanke told me of an offer he made to you yesterday which you refused. I asked you to come here to-day in order to beg of you to reconsider the matter. Mr. Milbanke and I are very anxious to do something for you."

At the words, Rossitur clenched the hand that rested on the table beside him. That she should want to do something for him in conjunction with Milbanke was an affront almost too great to be borne. But he mastered his anger and she went on.

"I have thought over every possible reason you can have for refusing, but I cannot find one that seems sufficient. Will you not give me the pleasure of telling Mr. Milbanke that you accept ?"

" No !" cried Rossitur, almost fiercely. " Not if I were starving ! Do you think, Lady Judith, that I have no pride, no self-respect ? And that *you* should wish me to

live at your husband's gate is past my com-
prehension! Is it possible that you cannot
forego the pleasure—or rather the triumph—
of seeing every day the man whose life you
have blighted? You can have what satisfaction you like out of my most miserable and
contemptible folly, but I tell you now, as I
have told you hundreds of times already—
and you know best how you responded—
that if I were to see you constantly I could
not answer for myself. Is not that enough
to justify my refusal?"

She made no answer, but taking up a letter
that was lying upon an open book beside her,
she tore off a blank page, and wrote a few
words upon it rapidly with the pencil that
hung from her waist-belt. In a minute or
two she had finished; and then, with a colour
on her cheek and a light in her eye such
as Milbanke had never seen, she threw the
paper across to Rossitur.

He read what she had written, twice;

looked up quickly, and met her eloquent
eyes fixed upon him.   A third time he read,
and then, without looking at her, he flung
the paper on the ground as if it had stung
him, and rose. " No, Lady Judith," he said,
" not even for *that !*   And I would give my
life if the inducement you hold out to me
there," and he pointed to the paper, "had
never entered your mind, or been put before
me in words—by—you."   His voice broke,
and he put up his hands before his face to
hide his emotion.

And as he stood thus, with, in his ear, the
voice of a subtle tempter urging him to give
way, he heard the rustle of her dress, and
presently the touch of her hand upon his
arm.

" Look at me," she whispered.   " You do
not mean what you say."

But once more she failed, and how he got
away from her she never knew ; but he had
shaken off her detaining hand, and was gone

without that look by which she hoped to conquer. She made a step or two forwards as if to recall him, but with a muttered "Too late!" she stopped short and seemed to listen. "Am I safe?" she said to herself. "If he betrays me all is lost."

Then she turned quickly, picked up the paper Rossitur had flung upon the floor, and tore it into tiny fragments. But she scattered them with such uncertain force that the greater part fell in a shower on the hearth-rug, and there she let them lie unheeded; it is even possible that she did not see them; her eyes were blinded with hot, angry tears; a stifled sob broke from her, and for a moment or two she covered her face, over which a deep, red flush had slowly spread, with her hands. In all her selfish, prosperous life she had never felt the pang of such bitter humiliation before.

"I wish he was dead!" she said. "With all my heart I wish he was dead."

And for himself, the man whom she had failed to tempt to his ruin echoed the wish, as, with his brain seemingly on fire, and his heart cold as death itself within him, he left her for ever, and found his way home, walking like one in a dream.

CHAPTER XVIII.

A WEEK OF PAIN.

DURING the week that elapsed between the departure of Milbanke from the farm and the day fixed for the wedding—it was to be celebrated with great pomp at the Parish Church of Stillingfort — Alice Rossitur watched her brother with great anxiety. He went about as usual, but it was plainly to be seen that, if not suffering mentally, as was too probable, he must be physically ill. His movements were languid; his eyes were heavy; his lips looked parched, he scarcely touched food; and as each night came on his head ached so intolerably—he confessed to so much being amiss—that he either lay on a sofa in his work room, with

his face turned from the light, or went to
bed.

But not to sleep. He admitted afterwards that during the whole of that wretched
week he had not slept for more than an hour
each night, and sometimes not even that
much. Alice could not get him to speak of
himself, but it seemed to her as if he were
quietly making preparations to leave Stillingfort.

While Milbanke was a prisoner at the
farm with his broken leg, Rossitur made
a special request to Ellen Balfour, the young
schoolmistress, to resume her practice on the
organ ; he gave her a lesson regularly every
other day, and she played for him twice at
the evening service. He was with her in the
organ loft in case she broke down, but Alice
heard him compliment her on her nerve and
the vigour of her touch at the close of the
service.

The day before the wedding he went to

the school and asked Ellen to be with him
during the ceremony. "I mean to play,
myself," he said, "if I can keep my fingers
on the keys, but I am so exhausted with
sleeplessness and pain that I may break
down at the last moment. You will not fail
me, Ellen?"

The girl looked up at him wistfully as he
laid his hand for a moment upon her shoulder.
Fail him! She would go to the end of the
world to serve him if necessary, and it made
her heart bleed to see how ill and worn he
looked. But even more alarming than his
haggard appearance was the dazed expression
in his eyes. One might imagine that he did
not actually see the objects at which he
looked.

"I am always glad to help you," she
answered, "but I wish we could persuade
you not to come to the church to-morrow;
you ought to take a long rest. Do allow
me to take all the responsibility, and if

I should break down, no one will notice it."

"No, no! We must not have any breaking down!" he exclaimed, in sudden excitement. "What may happen when all is over no one can tell. Something more than a break-down, perhaps, for I cannot bear this horrible agony much longer. But I must play the 'Wedding March' for the beautiful bride! I swore to myself that I would do it, and I mean to keep my word. How magnificent she will look in her white satin and orange blossom! You and I, Ellen, can see the ceremony from our high perch in the organ loft. I count upon you, remember, to be with me there."

"Choral service, I suppose?"

"Yes; full choral service. I was with the Vicar yesterday about it, and we had a practice last night."

"You might let me take the service," said Ellen, "and you can play the procession up

to the altar, and the 'Wedding March' as
they go out."

" ' The voice that breathed o'er Eden '—
they want that for the processional hymn,"
Rossitur said, without answering her request.
" What voice is it I wonder ?   And will it be
the same for the bridegroom and the bride ?
She will hear, perhaps, words of her own,
set to music, and he — but seeing will be
enough for him !   He ought to hear nothing
but the bride's ' I will !'   I am talking great
rubbish, am I not, Ellen ?   You are looking
at me out of those grey eyes of yours as if
you were afraid of me.   Grey eyes are softer
and kinder than dark eyes, child.   And more
pure and truthful ;   but not half — no, not
one half as lovely or as dangerous.   Tell me,
Ellen," he asked, presently, " do you see
writing on the walls ?   Everywhere I go I
see writing, and always the same.   There !
Look there !" and he pointed to the wall of
the schoolroom.   " I see five words written

in pencil in a woman's hand—'Come to be near me.' The farmer's son ought to have been proud to receive such an invitation. Now Ellen, look! the letters are turning red! Oh, will nothing blot them out? No; nothing but blood! Nothing but blood!"

It was the beginning of October then, and exquisite autumn weather. The woods were a mass of rich and varied colour, the sky was bright and clear, and the sun shone all day long. The village of Stillingfort was gaily decorated with triumphal arches and flags; the quaint old church, with its profusion of costly white flowers on the altar and in the chancel, looked a sanctuary fit to receive a young and lovely bride, and the school-girls, wearing white, were to scatter flowers before the happy pair as they walked from the porch to the carriage. The latter, drawn by four greys, was likely to attract as much attention and admiration as the bride herself.

The Park was full of guests; Lady Judith's

two brothers, Lord Warleigh and the Hon.
Rupert Forster, had arrived, and a host of
noble relatives on both sides of the house.
A dozen bridesmaids were to attend the
bride, and the beautiful and costly presents
she received were on view at the Park for
two days before the wedding.   Among them
was a very pretty riding-whip with a quaint
mounting and monogram in richly - chased
silver.   It was sent anonymously, and many
were the surmises as to the name of the
donor.   Lady Judith alone suspected Rossitur, for she recognised the monogram as one
he had designed for her in the early days of
their acquaintance, but she did not dare to
thank him for it ; and there it lay, a con-
spicuous, beautiful and unique object among
the other presents, and the words " giver
unknown " were on the paper attached to it.

Lady Judith had seen nothing of him since
their last meeting ; she told Mr. Milbanke
that she had used every argument in her

power to induce him to accept his offer, but
without success, and that a man so obstinately
blind to his own interests had better be left
alone. And there the matter dropped.
Milbanke felt that he had done all, and more
than all, that was required of him by gratitude,
and he would not subject himself to another
refusal.

When Dr. and Mrs. Murray came over
from Little Centre Bridge the day before the
wedding, the former was naturally very full of
the sad death of poor young Erskine, and of
the news the widow had sent home of his
faithful servant Pottinger.

" The poor fellow's people live in Stillingfort, I believe," the doctor said to his host,
and Lady Judith was present. " Do you
know anything about them ? Are they
tenants of yours ?"

" No ; not of mine. I may have heard
the name, but I do not recall it just now.
Out of his mind, did you say ? But that had

nothing to do with John Erskine's death, I
suppose."

"Oh, no! It was the effect of a severe
sunstroke, I believe ; but it was the shock of
seeing his master killed that upset him.   His
wife's people are your tenants, I know—the
Rossiturs."

"And a very cantankerous, troublesome
fellow old Rossitur is," said Lord Stillingfort.
"Nothing satisfies him, and I have done
more for him than for any other tenant on
the estate."

Lady Judith moved away soon after the
first mention of the name, and her father,
looking after her, said confidentially, "We
don't talk about those Rossiturs much here ;
the young fellow—he is our organist, you
know—had the presumption to fancy himself
in love with Judith, and gave me some
trouble.   But, fortunately, he has the good
sense to keep quiet now.   I must say these
fellows who are educated above their station

are a great nuisance, especially when they are good-looking. Very sad for Erskine to lose his son in that way. There is a little boy, is there not? And the widow is coming to the Chase, someone said. Has she arrived yet?"

"Not yet," Dr. Murray answered. "I believe she is going to winter abroad."

"Oh, indeed! We were abroad all last winter. It did not suit me very well, but My Lady liked it. Judith missed her hunting; but it was at Nice she met Milbanke, you know."

Dr. Murray knew, for he had heard it many times already.

"Most generous fellow, Milbanke. He has settled ten thousand a year pin-money on her, and if he were to die next week she would have five more. And when he got that bad fall and broke his leg the other day, he made his will and left her nearly every penny he had in the world. I am very glad he didn't die," his lordship added, "for, I believe, if she were independent, she would marry that organist fellow in spite of everyone."

"What an odd world it is," mused Dr. Murray to himself as, his conversation with Lord Stillingfort over, he watched the bearing of the bride and bridegroom elect towards one another. Her manner was as perfect to him as his to her. "Quite an ideal couple." "So devoted to one another." "A pity he is not a few years younger." Those were the general comments.

But in spite of their perfect accord and mutual satisfaction on the eve of their wedding-day, neither Lady Judith nor Mr. Milbanke could forget the young man who had so resolutely refused to accept any favour at their hands. He was the skeleton at their wedding-feast.

CHAPTER XIX.

SAVED.

THE marriage was arranged to take place at half-past eleven, as the bride and bridegroom were to leave by an early train in the afternoon for London *en route* for Paris ; and soon after ten the streets of the little town were filled to overflowing with sightseers who had flocked in from the neighbouring villages. The tenants on the estate, with their wives and daughters, mustered in force, as they were to be regaled with a big dinner in the afternoon in honour of the event.

The high road leading from the church to the Park gates was lined on either side with curious spectators, and soon after eleven the carriages of the neighbouring gentry, who had received invitations to the ceremony and to the wedding breakfast, began to drive up to the church in rapid succession. Ellen Balfour was busy long before eleven marshalling her little flock of school girls ; they all wore fresh white frocks and carried baskets filled with flowers.

Ellen herself looked pretty and modest in her soft gown of grey cashmere and white bonnet, but she was very pale and nervous, and her eyes were constantly straying to the path across the church meadows along which Charles Rossitur would come from the farm. His sister arrived in good time, and reported that he was coming but that he would not allow her to wait for him.

" He is worse than usual this morning, I am afraid," she said. " I listened at his door several times last night, and I could hear him talking to himself, and even laughing, in a

way that made my blood run cold to hear, for
I was afraid he was going to cut his throat or
shoot himself. When he came out to breakfast he said he was all right, but he did not
taste a mouthful and I am sure he will not be
able to play to-day."

While she was still talking of him he came
up, looking so handsome, but oh! so wofully
ill, Ellen thought. But he was perfectly
calm and collected ; in good spirits, a
stranger would have thought, for he said a
gay word or two to Ellen as he shook hands ;
laughed and joked with the little girls, and
took a white flower from the fullest basket to
fasten in the button hole of his black velvet
coat.

The villagers always said he was affected
in his dress, and he certainly did not look
very like the son of a farmer, in his loose
velvet coat, low turn - down collar and
carelessly knotted neckerchief of dark crim-
son silk. Perhaps it was that picturesque

Bohemian costume that first caught Lady Judith's fancy when he went to the Park to give her lessons on the organ.

As soon as he and Ellen Balfour had mounted to the organ loft, his mood changed. " I do not know how it will be when I feel my fingers on the keys," he said, as he unlocked and opened the instrument, " but I do not think I can play a note. My head aches so fearfully that I should just like to knock it against the wall yonder and quiet it for evermore. There! That is better," he added, presently as he seated himself and began to play. " There is nothing like music for chasing away or charming the evil spirits and the ghosts of the past. I wanted to come down here last night to try a voluntary that came into my head as I was lying awake. It went something like this." He began to play, but presently wandered off in a feeble, aimless manner and finally stopped. " I cannot do it," he said at last. "The inspiration went with the night."

"The choristers are coming in," said Ellen, who was looking over the curtain that hung in front of the loft. "Do you want the music of the hymn?"

"Of the wedding hymn? 'The Voice?'" he said. "Oh no! I could play it in my sleep. My sleep!" he said, dreamily. "I wonder if I shall ever sleep again. Yes; soundly to-night, when it is all over and she can never tempt me again, I shall sleep."

The words fell from him slowly, and in a half-whisper; but Ellen heard them only too distinctly, and a great terror came over her that he was going mad.

"Were you ever tempted, little Ellen?" he asked, presently, looking up with his beautiful, pathetic eyes. But there was something more than pathos in them that day; they were full of inarticulate pain. "Have you ever known what it was to have the happiness you have

dreamed of, and longed for with mad longing, put temptingly before your eyes, but,
between you and it, a slough of mud and mire
you would have to wade through before you
could grasp it? Not you, girl! Temptation
is a word in your dictionary, not in your life.
A thousand times a day I call myself an idiot
and a fool for resisting, and yet the mire and
dirt would surely have choked me some day.
But I did not hesitate a moment, Ellen;
remember that to my credit by and by. I
flung it from me and rushed out into dark-
ness, madness and despair!"

"I wish you would let me play and
you go home and lie down," she said, per-
suasively. "This dreadful pain is too much
for you."

"Only half-an-hour more, Ellen," he answered, "and then I shall lie down and rest,
and sleep too. But I must play the wedding
march as she goes out of church—a wife!
See; I am all right now. My fingers are quite

strong and steady. Let me have a peep at all the fine folk," he added, getting up and looking over the curtain. " What a lot of swells in pretty clothes! Ellen, what would they do if they had to walk through a pool of blood down there to their carriages? Or if it dripped down upon them as they passed out?"

" Oh, pray do not talk in that wild way!" cried Ellen, now seriously alarmed. " Where is Alice? I wish she was here."

" Never mind Alice; we do not want her. She is not quite like you, Ellen, and I am talking nonsense. My head is light for want of sleep, and there is the signal for me to begin. Tell me what you think of the bridegroom, Ellen. He is too old for her, but he is very kind and good. Now then." He began the hymn " The voice that breathed o'er Eden," and the choir began to sing as soon as the bride was inside the church.

Rossitur seemed calm now, and he asked

no more questions. Ellen stood looking over
the curtain, admiring, girl-like, the brilliant
throng, and the beautiful group formed by
the bride and her train of bridesmaids.

As soon as the ceremony began, Rossitur
left his seat and joined her; not a muscle of
his face moved as he listened to the exhor-
tation; but when it came to the bride's turn
to plight her troth he turned away with a
gesture incomprehensible to his companion,
and seated himself again at the organ.

"Come and stand by me with the Prayer
Book, Ellen," he whispered, "that I may
know when the 'Amen' comes in."

After that he went through his part of
the service without a mistake; but, when
the wedding party went into the vestry to
sign the register, he covered his eyes with
his left hand and sat motionless. Ellen
stood watching him, and she noticed that
his right hand was hidden in the inside
breast pocket of his coat. It was on that

spot she kept her eyes ; why, she hardly knew, but she fancied he was hiding something there.

Presently she whispered, "They are coming out. Can you play the March ?"

For one moment he looked at her with a puzzled expression as if he did not understand what she said, then he drew his hand from his pocket and began to play the well-known Wedding March as it had never been played in that church before. It was too fast and much too loud, and the reverberating chords echoed through the building. Lady Judith Milbanke looked up at the curtained gallery and wondered if he was alone there.

With a sudden break in the music the March ceased, and soft and low came a few bars of " With Verdure Clad." But that also broke off abruptly, and the exquisite melody " Oh, for the wings of a Dove," floated out and thrilled every ear with its unexampled sweetness.

"What is the organist about ? Is he mad this morning ?" said one guest to another down below.

Yes; what was he about, and was he mad? Entranced with the music she loved, Ellen forgot her fears ; but she was recalled to herself by a shock so appalling that to her dying day she never forgot it. With the cunning of madness—and he was mad, poor fellow, that day—Rossitur noticed her preoccupation; he continued to hold some chords with his left hand, while his right glided again to the pocket of his coat. The chords became discords, and, with her attention partially aroused, Ellen looked at him and at first noticed nothing except that he was pulling at his necktie as if it were choking him.

The next moment, with a cry for help that rang through the building, she flung herself upon him, and with all her strength fought with him for the open pen-knife he held in his hand. He had already given one wild gash to his throat, and if her slender fingers, nerved with the force of horror and despair, had not closed upon his, he would presently have lain dead at her feet.

At last, with one desperate effort, she wrenched the knife away; flung it high above the curtain, and heard it ring as it fell into the aisle below.

CHAPTER XX.

HOW IT ENDED.

BAFFLED in his attempt at self-destruction by the courage and determination of Ellen Balfour, Rossitur sank to the ground in a half-unconscious state. The violence of the paroxysm had passed, the terrible pressure on the brain being probably relieved by the flow of blood from his throat. It was not a serious cut, for the poor fellow's hand was nerveless, although when Ellen grappled with him for the knife, he rallied all his remaining strength to resist her.

The guests—men for the most part—who were waiting in the porch for carriages to come up, heard the cries for help, and before the frightened girl imagined that succour could reach her, half-a-dozen strange men were in the loft. They found her leaning exhausted against the organ ; her face was deadly white, while blood from her fingers, cut in the struggle for the knife, streamed over her dress. She had shut her eyes that she might not see Rossitur's agonised and ghastly face ; but she could not close her ears to the moans that now and then broke from him. It was evident that he was suffering intensely.

The doctor, quickly summoned, dressed the wound, which he declared was superficial and not at all likely to prove dangerous, but he said that the poor young fellow was in the first stage of acute brain fever, and would require the greatest possible care if his life was to be saved.

Ellen and his sister both testified to his late sufferings from sleeplessness, and the former added that his speech and bearing throughout the time she was with him in the organ loft that morning showed that his mind was unhinged. It was useless to declare now that he ought to have been kept away from the church, and indeed all needless regrets upon the subject were merged in the urgent question of the moment—how to get him home as quietly and with as little delay as possible.

It was done at last with infinite difficulty, and, as the speeches of congratulation were being made at the wedding breakfast, and the bride sat beside her husband, with her eyes demurely cast down as she listened to her own praises being sung, and to the reiteration of Milbanke's good fortune in having secured such a charming wife, poor Rossitur lay tossing on his bed with delirium coming on, and the fever increasing in intensity every moment.

The news of his sudden collapse, and the tragedy that had all but taken place in the church, spread like wildfire through the village, and was of course exaggerated by every tongue that repeated the story. The knife covered with blood, so one declared, had fallen on the bride's white gown, and left a great stain. She screamed at the ill-omened sight, and all but fainted in the bridegroom's arms. Another version, believed by many, was that the organist had fired a shot at the bridal party while the ceremony was proceeding, and that Lord Warleigh, the best man, would have been killed if he had not bent his head just in time to avoid the bullet. And a second shot would have followed the first if Ellen Balfour had not wrenched the pistol away.

Everyone said that everyone knew something dreadful would happen before long, Charles Rossitur had looked so unlike himself; and what had happened was a warning to young men not to fall in love with women who were above them in station. Was it likely that the Earl's only daughter would stoop to Farmer Rossitur's son?

The guests who had waited to assist in the removal of the unfortunate young man to his home, brought the news to the Park ; but, as it was such a horrible story for the bride to hear on her wedding-day, everything possible was done to keep it from Lady Judith's ears.

That something very unusual had taken place was, however, so patent to everyone that the bride's curiosity was aroused, and getting hold of her younger brother she made him tell her everything. And he did so in the matter-of-fact and unconcerned manner peculiar to a lad of about seventeen.

"Something happened after you left, you say ? By Jove! I should think so, rather ! That good-looking chap who plays the organ tried to stab himself or something, and he would have killed himself outright but for some plucky girl who was in the organ loft with him. She sang out for help, and seized the knife and got it from him, and flung it out into the body of the church. I believe it hit old Mulberry, the pew opener, on the top of his bald head and cracked it like a nut. I'm not joking! By Jove, Judy, you do look white! Have some fizz or something. I say, won't the *mater* pitch into me for telling you? They wanted to keep it dark, for fear you might think it unlucky!"

"Oh, never mind! I am all right," said Lady Judith. "But I wish it had not happened on my wedding-day. And they took him home, you say?"

"Yes; and the doctor says he's in for brain fever, poor chap. He was off his head, you know."

The bride was silent for a few minutes, and busy with the buttons of her glove. "Do you know who the girl was?" she said at last.

"No; not I. Never thought of asking. She is a plucky one, and no mistake."

No more was said, and when the happy pair had started, Lord and Lady Stillingfort congratulated themselves that Judith knew nothing of the catastrophe that had marred the splendour of her wedding-day.

And during the weeks that she was enjoying a luxurious honeymoon, with every wish, small or great, anticipated by her enamoured husband, and money at her command to gratify every whim, Rossitur was lying between life and death at Stillingfort.

Those only who watched him night and day, and heard his incessant ravings, and his wild appeals for help to resist some unknown temptation—which was either the delusion of a fevered brain, or one to which he had at some time been exposed—knew a tithe of his suffering.

Many and many a time did Alice and Ellen, who shared the nursing between them, wish that death would put an end to his trial and theirs. It was so pitiful to see the

strong young fellow lying there day after
day, either raving in wild delirium, or with
his mind wandering and his speech the
babble of a child. He recognised no one,
and the only thing that sometimes seemed to
soothe him was music.

Ellen used to play a familiar air softly on
the piano that stood at the far end of the
large room in which he lay ; but too often he
took no notice whatsoever, or tried to drown
the sound with his voice.

The days were growing short, and the
trees, those silent witnesses of secret meetings between the false woman and her
too credulous lover, were bare, and the late
flowers in the farm garden were black and
sere with early frosts, when Rossitur was
at last pronounced out of danger. The
change for the better came, as it so often
does, in a long sleep, and the two women
who loved him watched eagerly for his
awakening.

And when it came, he was once more in his right mind ; the storm of passion and despair that had beaten him down, and all but taken his life, was over, and he felt and spoke like a new man. As he grew stronger and better day by day he strove to recall his last hours of consciousness ; but his memory was treacherous and failed him utterly when he tried to remember what had happened before he awoke and found himself lying on his bed in his own familiar room, and so weak in body that he could scarcely raise his hand to his head.

When they told him that it was six weeks since he was taken ill he could scarcely be made to believe it, and it was only by very slow degrees that he was able to piece together scenes and events which, when he first began to recall them, seemed more like vague dreams than actual occurrences. As soon as he was out of danger Ellen Balfour gave up her share of the watching and nursing, and went back to her work at the school. She could not bring herself to wait for his recognition, for it would indeed be hard to bear should she see him turn from her now ; and she was, besides, honestly afraid lest the mere sight of her might recall the awful scene in the church too suddenly to his recollection, and cause a relapse ; so, as soon as he began to address those about him by name, she never went into his room, although she went to the farm every day to inquire after him.

If he remembered anything of the struggle between himself and her for the knife, he never spoke of it, and not once did Ellen's name pass his lips ; but his sister noticed that he used to watch the door incessantly, as if expecting someone to appear who never came.

When he was able to be up and about again Christmas was at hand, and the very first day he was able to walk as far he went straight to the school-house and surprised

Ellen by walking into her room as she sat
alone in the gloaming.

"Do you take me for a very tall, thin
ghost?" he said, as he went forward into
the circle of the bright firelight. "I am
afraid you do, you look so scared. You
would not come to see me, so I am obliged
to come and see you; but I think you are
rather unkind to neglect your handiwork as
soon as it is tolerably well patched up and
on its legs again."

"My handiwork!" was all she could
stammer in reply; emotion was choking
her, and to hide her confusion she got up
and made him take her chair by the fire.

She stood on the hearth with her eyes
fixed on the logs that were burning so
brightly and cheerily with vivid blue and
yellow flames; his eyes were fixed on her
pale, pure face.

"Ellen," he said, at last, and stretching
out his poor, thin hands he took one of hers

between them, " I want to thank you, my brave, true-hearted, little friend, for having saved my life. It has taken me a very long time to remember what happened on Lady Judith's wedding-day, but I have got it all plain and clear now, and I owe it to you that I did not kill myself like a coward. I can but hope that this strong little hand," and he raised it to his lips as he spoke, " has given back to the world of workers a safer and more sensible man than the man who tried to play the organ that day. What do you say, Ellen? You have not much hope of me, I am afraid, or you would speak," he added, as he drew her towards him by the hand he still held.

" It is not that—I always had hope of you," she faltered. " It is because I am so glad to see you well again."

" Yes ; well again. Well in mind, thank God. And it is not only the madness of the fever that has passed—another and a more

pestilent fever has died out, and the wild
desire and mad longing of the past two years
have disappeared with it, and a desire that is
better and nobler, and more fit for such a man
as I am, has been born again.   Ellen, I am
ashamed to remember that more than two
years ago, in this very room, and seated in
this spot, I gave you to understand, although
I did not say so in words, that I cared for
you, not as a brother or as a friend, but as a
lover; and yet, from that hour until this, no
word of love for you has passed my lips.   I
need not tell you how I was drawn away from
you, or by whom, for you know all; and in
your heart perhaps you despise me for a poor
weak fool, but——"

"Oh! no—no!" broke from her involuntarily, and pulling her hand from his detaining
clasp she covered her agitated face and burst
into convulsive sobs.

In a moment he was by her side with his
arm round her.   "Ellen—my dearest," he

whispered, "Do not turn from me. I love you—you will always be to me the noblest, truest and sweetest woman on earth. If you ever cared for me, oh! care for me now when I so sorely need your love. Be my wife, and let us go away together out of this hateful place. Will you—will you come?"

"I will go with you to the end of the world!" she answered, as she threw herself weeping upon his breast.

CHAPTER XXI.

WHEELS WITHIN WHEELS.

THE winter passed very quietly at Little
Centre Bridge. In consequence of their
deep mourning the family at the Chase went
nowhere and received no company. It was
rather a dreary and monotonous life for a
young girl like Letty, but she did not feel it
irksome or wish for any change. She read a
great deal, and the books she chose were not
chiefly novels, but standard works she had
heard Otway speak of when they were first
acquainted. She also got her friend Dr.
Murray to recommend her some improving
literature, while in fiction and poetry she was
careful to select those writers only whom she
knew Otway admired and approved. His

literary palate was very fine, and she could
not do better, she thought, than be guided by
his taste.   It did not matter, or she told herself it did not, that no opportunity would
probably ever offer itself for the discussion
with him of the various volumes, grave and
gay, that went backwards and forwards that
quiet winter between the Chase and Mudie's.
Letty satisfied herself by reading books that
she knew were well known to him.

Then she and her father took long rides
and walks together.   Sir John was not a
specially intellectual companion, but still he
and his daughter had many subjects in
common, and the subject of his little grandson Jack, was a never-failing source of
interest and speculation to the old man.
Occasionally he recurred to the vexed question of the relations between Letty and her
husband, and declared with great emphasis
that they ought either to come to an under-
standing or else have the marriage annulled ;

but Letty generally contrived to impress upon
him that she was quite satisfied to let things
remain as they were.

Mrs. John Erskine had had her way, and
was spending the winter at Sorrento with her
own child ; Rossitur the maid, and Rossitur's
boy. No one knew exactly how the thing
had been managed and Sir John's strong
repugnance to the scheme overcome ; but
the fact was, Mrs. John simply offered
passive resistance, and to all her father-in-
law's arguments in favour of her immediate
return to England replied that she thought it
was better for her and the child to spend the
winter in a warm climate.

A second letter had immediately followed
her first from Simla ; and in it she announced
that before an answer to it could be received
she should be on her way to Europe. A
letter addressed to her on board the P. and
O. steamer *Cathay*, at Suez, would probably
find her, but it might perhaps be safer to

write to " Poste Restante, Naples," as she
meant to go there direct from Brindisi.

On receipt of this communication, which
showed that Mrs. John Erskine was by no
means a 'feckless' creature, unable to manage
her own affairs, and was certainly not disposed, as far as her friends at the Chase could
judge, to let others manage for her, Sir John
telegraphed at once to Simla, and said she
was to look for a letter at Suez but not at
Naples, as he hoped his "dearest Amy"
would be guided by him, and instead of
landing at Brindisi come on direct to South-
ampton or to London, where he and Letty
would meet her and escort her home.

And at Suez a long letter met her con-
veying the same desire expressed at length.
Sir John was a diffuse letter writer, who
always gave his reasons *in extenso*, and often
many times over, for the course he meant to
take upon himself or to impose upon others ;
the *pros* and *cons* were minutely gone into,

and often repeated in another form of words.
He explained elaborately to his daughter-in-
law that, in his opinion, she ought to lose no
more time than was absolutely necessary in
bringing her orphan boy to the home that
would one day be his. "You have a certain
position to take up in the county, my dear,"
he wrote, "and the sooner it is taken up the
better. Indeed, I may say without exaggera-
tion, that you are *being waited for in Stoneshire*, and a warm and most loving welcome
will be given to you, not only by me, your
sister, and your Aunt Louise, but by all
the inhabitants, gentle and simple, of Little
Centre Bridge."

Then he dilated at large upon the dangers
of ill-drained Italian towns, and declared that
it would be altogether against his wishes if
his grandson spent even a night in Italy.

"What a tiresome, twaddling, old creature
he must be," was Mrs. John's comment as
she read the lengthy epistle aloud to her

maid; it was the least she could do when
Rossitur helped her so cleverly with her own
compositions.

"One would think that Jack was the only
child in the world, he makes such a fuss
about him.   I think myself he is a very
ordinary child; but of course, the heir of all
the Erskines must be something extraordinary to the Erskines.   If Sir John only
knew how I detest the idea of going to the
Chase he would be astonished.   Fancy being
stared at and talked over by all the Little
Centre Bridgeians !"

"You might get some amusement out of it
all for a while, madam," Rossitur answered ;
it was a matter of indifference to her where
her mistress spent the winter.   "I have been
told that the Chase is a very fine place, and
that everything is done on a liberal scale.
Sir John's servants always stay with him a
long time."

"It is more than his daughter-in-law will

do," Mrs. John answered.   "I mean to
amuse myself by and by, and I ought to
be presented next spring.   Poor Captain
Erskine always meant to have it done"—
Amy spoke of her appearance at court as she
might have spoken of a surgical operation
to remove some physical blemish—"when
we came home on leave. I think I had better
telegraph as soon as we get to Malta"—this
conversation took place on board the *Cathay*
—"to say I am not coming to England, and
that he must write, as I told him before, to
Poste Restante, Naples.   It is very easy, if I
do not like either Naples or Sorrento, to go
to England overland ; but I am determined
to spend the winter in Italy if I can."

"I hope it will not be too lonely for you,
madam," Rossitur said, "but you may find
someone you know at Sorrento."

Mrs. Erskine hesitated a moment before
she said, carelessly, "Monsieur de Louvain's
mother and sister have a villa at Sorrento"

—Rossitur was quite aware of that fact—
"and they seem disposed to be friendly,"

"Indeed, madam? That is good news.
Do they know you are coming?"

"Oh! dear, yes. I had a letter at Suez to
say that they have taken an apartment for us
in such a charming situation, and Monsieur
de Louvain will meet me at Brindisi. It is
very good of him."

"Very, indeed, madam," and Rossitur bit
her lip to hide her significant smile.

"And now, what do you think, Rossitur?
Of course I do not want to make any unnecessary mystery, but Sir John is so pre-
judiced against foreigners and foreign places
that I think it would be just as well not to
mention the de Louvains when we write.
He need not know anything about my
acquaintances in Sorrento ; and if these
people mean to be nice and friendly why
should I not meet them half-way? What do
you say?"

"Certainly, madam ; and there is no necessity for you to mention them. I am sure I am very glad to know that you are going to meet such an old friend as Monsieur de Louvain again."

"And his mother and sister as well, you know. I am looking forward with *quite* as much pleasure to meeting them."

"Naturally, madam."

"How do you think I am looking now, Rossitur ? Do you know, I am afraid I am getting stout. There is scarcely any difference in our figures now, is there ? I used to be always such a thin girl, and you were always plump. But you do not think I am disfigured at all, do you, Rossitur ?"

"Not at all, madam. I do not think I ever saw you looking better. A little tanned by the sea air, but that will soon wear off at Sorrento, and Monsieur de Louvain knows how fair you are naturally. He many and many a time talked of your beautiful complexion to me when you were a young lady at Calcutta."

"Heigh ho!" said Amy, with a sigh. "What gay times we had then! Hadn't we, Rossitur? I often think I was foolish to marry so young; but poor dear Captain Erskine was so nice-looking——"

"And better off than any of your admirers, madam," put in the maid.

"And better off than any of them, as you say; and of course I could not tell that another person would come in for a fine estate just after I married."

"Is that so, madam?"

"Yes," with another sigh. "But then, if my poor dear husband had lived, I should have been Lady Erskine some day; and after all, an old English baronetcy is not to be despised, is it Rossitur? And Lady Erskine is a pretty title; much prettier than plain Mrs. John. I should not in the least mind changing *that* if I got a chance. By

the way, Rossitur, talking of husbands reminds me, have you had any news lately
of Pottinger? We have to think about him
now, as we are getting near England."

"He was getting better when last I heard,"
Rossitur answered, "and the doctor thought
that in a few months he would be quite well
again."

"Then we need not trouble about him for
six months, at least, need we? When we
get home next year I suppose you will let
your own people have your little Georgy to
take care of. I am afraid I cannot ask Sir
John to take him in at the Chase."

"Oh! dear; no, madam! But if Pottinger
recovers I suppose he will expect me to go
and live with him."

"Oh, but I really cannot part with you
now, Rossitur! You know all my little ways
so well I should be lost without you! I am
sure I could not have written all those letters
to Sir John without your help, you are such

a famous scribe! No, no! Pottinger must go back to the regiment and leave you with me. I know you will not break your heart about him. You see now the folly of engaging yourself before you left England. I might have come out to India engaged, but I would not hear of it. It ties one down so, doesn't it, Rossitur?"

"Certainly it does, madam."

"I wonder what Sir John will say when he hears I am not coming home for the winter. We must concoct a very nice letter and smooth him down. I do not want him to come out to Italy to look after me."

"He is too much afraid of the smells," said Rossitur. "But if he talks of it we must find some way of putting him off."

"Yes; we must indeed. I leave it all to you, Rossitur; you are so clever at inventing!"

And at that compliment to her powers, Rossitur laughed and made no reply.

CHAPTER XXII.

THUS were all Sir John's plans and wishes quietly set aside by the determination of an obstinate and decidedly selfish young woman to have her own way. He got her telegram from Malta and her letter from Brindisi, such a sweet, prettily worded, dutiful letter, for the most part the work of Rossitur's fertile brain. Composition was generally an arduous task to young Mrs. Erskine, and it was never more difficult than immediately after her arrival at the Italian port where she was met and welcomed not only by her old friend Victor de Louvain, but also by his sister who had accompanied him from Sorrento

But in the letter that reached the Chase announcing the arrival of the little party, there was no mention made of their kind and thoughtful friends.

Sir John was in a pretty fume when he found that he must wait until spring to see his son's widow and her boy ; and endless were the woes he poured into the ears of his friend, Dr. Murray, on the subject. But the Doctor, like a sensible man, contrived to put Mrs. John's apparent wilfulness in a reasonable light. He said it was not possible to expect her to enter fully into her father-in-aw's impatience to embrace his grandson, and to welcome the widow of his lost son.

" She naturally wishes to spend a few months in perfect seclusion, poor thing," the good Rector said. " She shrinks, you may rest assured that she shrinks, from the excitement inseparable from her home-coming under these sadly altered circumstances. It is just as well for you to humour her, Erskine

Just as well. Her heart must be sorely bruised and bleeding, poor girl, and nothing will help her so much as quiet."

"But she will be so lonely; and think of the smells," Sir John persisted; but he felt that the ground was being cut from under his feet.

"Oh! the smells are exaggerated, and, believe me, loneliness is just what she is pining for, or she would have come home at once; and the time will soon pass. I am sure her rooms at the Chase are not ready for her yet, although you are in such a hurry; or those wonderful nurseries for Master Jack. You are not thinking of buying a pony for him yet, I suppose? By-the-way, how old is he?"

"He was born a week or two before Letty was married; he will be two years old when he comes home if she brings him in March. I think, if I give in about the winter, I ought to insist upon March."

" What about the east winds after Italy ?"

" Oh—bother Italy! I wish there was no such place! And, you know, we hardly ever have the east wind in Stoneshire. Oh, no. I must insist upon March, and then we can have a nice quiet summer here. Amy will not care to see any company, of course, except just a few old friends ; and Herbert Otway, I know, wants to make her acquaintance."

" I saw him, by the bye, when we were in town last week," said the Rector. " He wanted us to dine with him at Rutland Gate, but we had not time. That is where he took the house when he married, I suppose ?"

" Yes ; that is the place. I wonder," after a pause, " what could be done to reconcile those two?"

" I am afraid the thing has gone too far now," answered the Rector. " I cannot help thinking that if he were in love with her still he would not go on month after month in this way. It is unnatural, to say the least of it. By and by, you will see he will propose to have the marriage annulled. A friend of mine whom I met in town, and who knows him very well, told me the other day that he has lately been left trustee to a very handsome widow who is supposed—mind, I only say 'supposed'—to have jilted him for the rich man she afterwards married, and who has now left her with a pot of money."

"Is her name Ogilvey?" cried Sir John.

"Yes; that is it. Do you know her?"

"I surprised her once in his chambers, and he said she was a client; it was before he was married, of course. Now, Murray, not a word of this to Letty. Let us wait and see what happens."

During the winter there were letters once a fortnight, and sometimes oftener, from the Villa Lucia at Sorrento. They were not very long letters, nor were they specially interesting, for, by her own account, Mrs.

John Erskine led the quietest and most uneventful of lives. The weather was charming, but still the climate of Italy did not quite come up to its reputation ; and it was curious, and rather provoking, too, that the winter in England should be so unusually mild that year. There were no English families at Sorrento that season, with the exception of a consumptive clergyman from Yorkshire called Beauchamp Jones and his wife and two very plain daughters. Mrs. John understood from Rossitur, who had picked up a little Italian, and had heard all about the family from the laundress, of all people in the world, that the Joneses, poor people, had left seven other daughters at home in the Yorkshire Rectory.

Little Jacky was growing very fast, his dear grandpapa would be glad to hear ; but he was not like either his darling father or her, and he was slow at speaking; and so also was Rossitur's boy, little Georgy Pottinger.

Mrs. John wondered if being born in India had anything to do with it.

Just after Christmas there was rather a long break in the correspondence, and when at last a letter came it was full of the tragedy that had all but happened at Lady Judith Forster's wedding.   Alice had written to her sister Bella, and told her all about their brother's attempt upon his life in the church while he was in the act of playing the wedding party down the aisle, and of his illness, recovery and engagement to Ellen Balfour the schoolmistress.

" Rossitur is in despair," Mrs. John concluded, "not only at the commonplace ending to it all, but also because he is throwing himself away upon such a girl ; and they have actually made up their minds to go to Australia.   He has got the post of organist in one of the Melbourne churches."

" I think," said Letty, when the letter was read, "that Amy might not treat us to the Stillingfort news. Does she imagine that we do not know all about Judith's marriage? By-the-way, the Milbankes were at Naples the other day, and they are in Rome now."

The end of February came, and then Mrs. Erskine, of her own accord, fixed the time for her arrival in England, and Sir John could not contain his joy. Letty and Miss Lambton did not anticipate the coming of the young widow and her son with such lively satisfaction, and although they did not speak of their doubts to one another, each was convinced in her own mind that Mrs. John's presence would have the effect of breaking up once for all the quiet home-life of the Chase.

Another letter somewhat quickly followed the one wherein Mrs. Erskine announced that on such and such a day she meant to start for England; and it contained news so unexpected, and of such importance to all concerned, that it will be given in the writer's own words.

" What do you think, dearest Sir John, Letty and Aunt Louise ? Can you believe it ? ROSSITUR HAS LEFT ME!!! I can scarcely believe it myself although I am on the spot, but she is gone ! Actually GONE!!! And what I am to do without her I do not know. I never expect to have my hair properly dressed again, and as to finding any of my things — it is hopeless ! We had a disagreement and she said she wished to go, and of course I could not ask her to stay, and so she went. I consider that she has treated me in the *most* heartless and ungrateful manner after my *years* of kindness, and the way I stood by her, I may say fought for her, when she nearly got into a serious scrape just before her marriage to that poor Pottinger. And what a bad wife she made him—but that is neither here nor there, is it ? My poor darling never liked her, I must say

that, and if he had had his way she would
not have been with me very long after I
married. But he saw how useful she was, so
he never interfered about her a second time.
Oh, my darling husband! If I only had you
now! Well; it all came about in this way.
I had my Ayah here all the winter, and she
took the *entire* charge of the two children—
mine and Rossitur's — but when she went
away (I sent her back a fortnight ago) I
proposed to Rossitur that, as soon as we got
to England, she should settle her boy with
her sister at Stillingfort, and then come back
to me and act as my maid and little Jack's
nurse. Now, was there anything very unreasonable in that? She could have done
the double work perfectly, and I did not like
to arrive at the Chase with two servants in
my train. But my lady was highly offended
at being asked, and said she would attend
upon me as usual, but that she did not like
taking care of children and would have noth-

ing to do with my darling pet. I got a little vexed, perhaps ; but she was really very impertinent—as she can be when she likes— and the upshot is that she went the very next day. But where she went to I have not the faintest notion. I am afraid she is up to no good, for I noticed a curious change in her of late.

" Now, as soon as I get to London, I am going to look out for a nice, steady girl, who will act as my maid and Jack's nurse. He is getting bigger and older every day, and he will soon be past nurses ; besides, I am sure dear Letty or Aunt Louise, would not mind looking after him sometimes when the girl was engaged with me ; or there might be a housemaid without much to do—that was what I said to Rossitur—and I really do not want so very much done for me, as you will see. I am *very* curious to know if that woman has gone home. Could you find out quietly by and by ? I am sure she has not.

She is very deep. My darling Jack always said she was very deep, and I am sure now he was right. As soon as you get my telegram from the Grand Hotel to say I am there, come up at once and take me home. I feel *I shall never be happy until I have seen you all.*"

Sir John looked quite radiant as he finished the letter. "I must go and tell Murray," he said.

"What do you think of the latest news?" he exclaimed, as he walked without ceremony into Dr. Murray's study. "Amy writes to say that Rossitur is gone. Think of that. Rossitur is gone!"

CHAPTER XXIII.

"Mrs. Murray is going to London to shop
to-morrow, and she wants me to go with
her," Letty announced one afternoon when
she came in from her drive. It was now
nearly the end of the first week in March,
and Sir John was in daily expectation of a
telegram from his daughter-in-law to say that
she was in London.

"The Doctor went to town this morning,"
he said.

"Yes ; he had to go up on business, and
he is to meet us to-morrow at Blanchard's at
two o'clock for luncheon. We expect to get
back here by the 8-15 train. Aunt Louise,
have you any commissions ?"

"Oh yes, dear ; I want a few little things
if it will not bore you.   Shall I make a little
list ?   And then if you cannot get what I
want, never mind.   But you are sure to be in
Bond Street and Regent Street.   If you
could get me a pretty mourning-cap at
Ludlow's ; or two, if you see any that will
suit me."

"All right, auntie.   You want to look
your smartest when Amy comes ?"

"I wonder if she would be hurt to see
a little bit of lavender on my head ?   But
perhaps it is better to have all black just at
first.   One never knows how people will take
things."

"Do you want anything, papa ?"

"You might look in at Jackson and
Graham's, and ask them when I am to have
that writing-table I ordered for Amy's room.
I want it to be here when she comes.   And
you might get some of those Indian rugs
and mats and things at Liberty's.   They will

make the place look home-like to the poor
child."

" I notice that people who have been in
India hate those things," said Letty.   " But
never mind ; if Amy does not care for them,
Auntie and I will be very glad to have them,
so let them come.   Is that all you want ?"

" Perhaps you will not object to take that
to spend on fal-lals for yourself," said Sir
John, as he pulled out a five pound note and
gave it to Letty.   " I'll bet a guinea you are
hard up."

" I am not hard up as it happens," answered
Letty, laughing, "but I am very glad to get
this, all the same.   I do not expect to have
as many presents now that Amy is coming."

" I am astonished we do not hear from
her," said Sir John,   " Poor thing !   I am
afraid she finds it hard to get on without that
woman, Rossitur.   By the way, did I tell
you that I asked Murray to find out through
the curate at Stillingfort if she was at her

father's, but nothing has been seen or heard of her ?"

" I am very glad she is not coming here," said Letty. " I took a great dislike to her ; I believe, because poor, dear Jack had no faith in her."

It was a bright, and for March, a warm morning, when Mrs. Murray and Letty left by an early train for London, and they had finished the greater part of their shopping before two o'clock, the hour fixed for luncheon at Blanchard's. They met punctually, and sat down a merry little trio, but Letty's gaiety was suddenly and utterly quenched by the unexpected appearance of Otway, who came in accompanied by a lady in the dress of a widow.

Dr. Murray, who was speaking to her at the moment, saw the bright colour rush into the girl's cheeks, and with a quick movement she drew down her veil. Glancing at his wife, the Doctor saw that she was attracted by some new arrivals, and looking over his shoulder, he saw the pair who had just seated themselves at a table in the middle of the room, and heard Otway asking for the *menu*.

"Take no notice, please," said Letty, quietly. "We can finish our luncheon and go out without being recognised."

But if she had had any enjoyment in her luncheon before, she had none now ; she said a word at random now and then, and did her best to understand what her companions were talking about, and as she tried to listen to to them, she made a series of most determined efforts to keep her eyes from straying to that other table, and the face of the handsome woman who seemed on such friendly terms with *him !* She was not young ; Letty felt an almost spiteful satisfaction in the conviction that she must be at least forty ! But then, what young girl was ever so dignified in manner—so perfectly

self-possessed, and with that unmistakable
stamp upon her that marks the woman of the
world.

" How well she seems to talk," thought
poor Letty to herself. She could not but
note the fact that Otway listened attentively,
and laughed now and then as if he were well
amused.

" I could not entertain him as she does,"
Letty went on with her unspoken comments.
" The twaddle of a country town must seem
very tame to him after that sort of thing ;
and yet, he said to me once, that to hear me
calling my chickens to be fed was like the
sweetest music in his ears. Ah ! he was in
love then !"

All this time Otway's back only was
visible, and he seemed to be enjoying his
luncheon and the conversation of his companion.

" Are you going to speak to him ?" Mrs.
Murray asked, addressing her husband, as

they all rose and were about to leave the room.

"Oh, no ; I think not, my dear. He will probably not see us. But perhaps Letty would like——"

"I would rather not, thank you. Much rather," was Letty's prompt reply. "Let us get out. It is so hot here."

The Rector led the way ; his wife followed, and they both passed close behind Otway without being seen by him. Letty came last. Her heart began to beat very fast as she got near that special table, and found the eyes of the handsome widow fixed upon her glowing face. How far away the door seemed. Should she never reach it? The fates were against it apparently. First she tripped against the leg of a chair that was a little tilted, and too far out. The man who occupied it was in the act of drinking, and, feeling the jar, he began to choke, and coughed violently while he rose and tried to apologise for being in the way.

Letty, wishing him at Jericho and herself in the street, hurried on ; but fearing that his chair might be in the way, Otway had risen also, and she found herself suddenly face to face with him.

"Are you alone?" he said, as he held out his hand. She was obliged to give him hers and he held it while he waited for her answer, and held it firmly too.

"Oh, no!" she said. "I am with the Murrays. They went out this moment, and they are waiting for me downstairs."

He dropped her hand at once. "Remember me to Sir John and Miss Lambton," he said.

She passed on and he sat down again.

"Do you mean to say that you were speaking to your wife?" Mrs. Ogilvey said, across the table. "She is scarcely as pretty as she was, is she?"

" I really do not know. I did not notice particularly," answered Otway, carelessly, and turned the conversation.

" Well, dear," said Mrs. Murray, as Letty joined her. " What kept you so long ?"

" Oh! I knocked up against a chair, and the man who was on it nearly choked himself with his claret, and Mr. Otway saw me, and asked if I was alone ; that is all. Who is that lady who is with him, Dr. Murray, do you know ?"

" I think her name is Ogilvey, my dear. Fine woman, is she not ? She lost her husband lately."

Ogilvey! Letty remembered the name well enough.

" I do not admire her," she answered, shortly. And then she and Mrs. Murray began to discuss their plans for the afternoon.

" By six o'clock the two ladies reached Victoria Station, where Dr. Murray was to meet them in time for the 6-30 train to Little Centre Bridge.

"We are too soon, of course," said Letty. "Come into the waiting-room and let us try and put our parcels together or something will be left behind."

When they went into the ladies' room they found the woman - in - charge and several ladies in a high state of excitement. The former held in her arms a child of about a year and a half or two years old. It was neatly and comfortably dressed, and it did not seem in the least put out by all the strange faces about it. It held out its little arms now to one and now to another, and said "ma-ma," and then, with the pretty coquetry of a baby, it would hide its face on the attendant's shoulder, and give a little peep out now and then.

"Oh, what a sweet little boy !" Mrs. Murray exclaimed. She was a baby-worshipper, pure and simple, and never as happy as when she had a child in her arms. " Look, Letty! Such a little darling! Whose is he?" she added, addressing the woman. " Yours?"

" Oh, dear no, ma'am. He is nothing to me. About two hours ago a lady, at least she seemed like a lady—she had a veil on so I could not see her face, but I am sure she was young—came in with this child in her arms, and she carried a good-sized bag, too. She put the bag down on the seat over there, and then put the child beside it, and after talking to it for a bit, and feeding it with cake, she says to me, ' I am just going into the refreshment room for a sandwich and a glass of ale, will you have an eye to this little fellow until I come back? He's very good, and I shan't be long. Bye-bye——" I think she said some name, but I did not catch it rightly, and off she went. Well, I kept an eye on the child, and he did not cry or fret, but at the end of a quarter-of-an-hour

I began to wonder his mother did not come back. I wondered more at the end of half-an-hour what had become of her, and I just took the child in my arms and went to look for her. But she was gone, and they told me in the refreshment room that no one answering to her description had been there for a glass of ale, and my belief is that it was all a trick to get rid of the child."

"Oh, what a horrid woman!" broke from some of the ladies, and with great emphasis from Mrs. Murray. "Such a sweet little boy! How could your mother desert you, poor little darling?" she added, as she kissed the little fellow.

"But what are you going to do with him?" Letty inquired. "Keep him until you see if the woman will come back?"

"Oh, she won't come back no more, she won't, bless you!" the attendant answered. "She's not the first of the sort I've seen. But somehow, I wasn't thinking of a trick,

or I'd have dodged her. I've been talking
to one of the inspectors, and he's going to
fetch a policeman to take the poor little chap
to the workhouse. Seems a pity, doesn't
it? That's his bag there, as I looked over.
There's a tidy lot of his clothes in it, and a
little comb and brush and a sponge, but no
name or address or anythink."

" Oh, it is dreadful to think of his going to
the workhouse!" cried Mrs. Murray. " Let
me take him home with me."

" My dear Mary," cried Letty.

" Yes, dear; why not? I am sure the
doctor will let me. I can leave my name
and address with the station-master, and then
if the mother comes to look after him she can
get him back. We will pay her expenses,
of course. Just let me find my husband; he
must be waiting for me outside."

Dr. Murray, who would probably have
allowed his wife to bring a young elephant
home had she wished it, gave his consent

after a few trivial objections; and the more
readily as he was sure, if none of the women
were, that the child's mother would re-appear
and claim it the following day at the latest.
The arrangement took trouble and responsibility off their shoulders, so the officials had
nothing to say against it, and Mrs. Murray
had her way and carried off the child in
triumph.

And during the journey home she was
never tired of calling the attention of her
companions to his many perfections. "And
I am quite sure he is not a common child!"
was her refrain after every remark.

"I wonder what the people will say when
they hear you have brought home a baby,
my dear!" the doctor said, as they were
steaming into Little Centre Bridge Station.
"I am glad Letty can bear witness that he is
a waif picked up at Victoria Station. I do
not want a sensational paragraph to get into
the *Stoneshire Mercury*."

" A waif indeed ! As if waifs had ever such well-kept hair, and such dear little hands. I am quite sure he is not a common child !"

Letty, of course, was the first to carry the news to the Chase that the Rector's wife had gone to London to shop and had brought back a baby. She made very merry over the incident, but she was in a somewhat cynical mood at the close of that eventful day.

CHAPTER XXIV.

TAKEN AT HIS WORD.

NOT since Letty Erskine had come back to her home, a bride but not a wife, had the gossips of Little Centre Bridge such a treat. It was known at "Crump's" very early the following morning, that Mrs. Murray had brought back a little boy from London ; and Mrs. Sumner, who chanced to drop into the shop for a set of knitting pins soon after breakfast, heard from Mrs. Crump herself that Dr. and Mrs. Murray had some time ago advertised for a child to adopt, and out of half-a-dozen or more babies submitted for their. approval they had selected this particular boy.

When Mrs. Verity told her husband about

it, that excellent man and shrewd lawyer was
guilty of the extreme vulgarity of putting his
thumb to the end of his nose, and of giving
a highly suggestive wink with his left eye.
" Very good story, my dear," he said, " but
my friend, the doctor, cannot bamboozle me!"

It was extremely difficult for the Murrays
to get the true version of the story believed
in the town, although they had Letty's
evidence to back it up ; and poor Mrs.
Murray was quite weary at last of exhibiting
the child to her visitors, and of reiterating
her conviction that its mother would soon
re-appear to claim it. But she did not
appear, and it was extraordinary how, in the
short space of four - and - twenty hours, the
little fellow had contrived to enslave the
household at the Rectory. Master, mistress
and servants were all led captive by his
pretty. ways, and his sweet baby face, with
its big brown eyes, and the little head
covered with fair, fluffy curls. Mrs. Murray

was sure if her own baby boy had lived he
would have been just such a dear, pretty,
gentle, good-tempered little fellow, and she
had already extracted a promise from her
indulgent husband that, if the mother did
not come back, she might keep the child
instead of sending him to an orphanage, or
to be " boarded out " with a farmer's wife in
the parish.

Three uneventful days passed after the
visit to London. Letty was unusually silent,
if not sad ; she could not banish the remem-
brance of that handsome and fascinating
Mrs. Ogilvey ; but neither could she forget
the close, warm pressure of Otway's hand,
although she could not understand why he
held it so long. It must have been done in
a fit of absent-mindedness, for, of course, he
could not have cared to hold it.

Sir John during those days of waiting was
very fidgety and impatient ; giving orders
and countermanding them in a breath, while

Aunt Louise, as usual, sympathised with and listened to everyone in turn.

At last the long-expected news came. Mrs. John Erskine was in London. She wrote as follows from the Grand Hotel— " You will be glad to hear, dearest Sir John, that I am actually in England with my precious boy. We arrived from Paris early this morning ; had a most charming crossing. I was not the least ill, and the little man behaved beautifully. I travelled alone the whole way, and I am very proud of myself for having got on so well. I was sorry, when I found myself actually on my way, with no one to help me, that I had not asked you to send over a footman to escort me ; or I am sure Herbert Otway, who is a sort of brother-in-law of mine, you know — his brother married my half-sister—would have fetched me. However, here I am all right, and I hope you will come up at once and take me home. I have nothing to keep me here,

except to get a maid who will act as Jacky's
nurse as well. One of the chambermaids
here is very kind in looking after him for me.
I want the address of Letty's *modiste*, for
I am really so shabby I am quite ashamed to
show myself! You were kind enough to say,
dearest Sir John, that I might take *carte
blanche* for the replenishing of my wardrobe
when I got to London, so I have already
ordered a black silk dress for the afternoon,
at Jay's, elegantly trimmed with crape and
jet, and a charming mantle to go with it.
I desired them to send the bill—forty-five
pounds—to you. Forty-five for the two. I
am so much obliged to you, dearest Sir John.
I enclose in this a bill for a set of beautiful
jet ornaments I gave myself in Paris with
your love. I knew you would like me to
have them ; and as soon as I finish this I am
going out to get a present from you for your
little Jacky. He is so shabby, poor little
mite, and he must look very smart when

he gets to his dear grandpapa's, where every-one will look at him. In fact he wants *everything ;* and I must get a couple of pretty bonnets for myself, and something *very* sweet in hats to travel in, and for country wear ; and I want you to come with me to your tailor and help me to order the very newest thing in summer ulsters—something I can walk about in ; and I must get a pretty travelling-cloak at Redfern's. That is the best place, is it not ?

"This hotel is charming ! I have such a pretty sitting-room off my bedroom on the first floor. I knew you would not like me to go into the coffee-room, and I have arranged with the manager for a carriage by the day. He is most civil and obliging. He seemed to know your name quite well."

"I do not think he ever heard it in his life !" growled Sir John, to whom, it must be confessed, his daughter - in - law's letter was rather a startling revelation. But he was not going to admit anything of the kind ; he had a suspicion that both Letty and Miss Lambton were disposed to criticise Mrs. John's proceedings rather freely if he gave them an opening ; and, as he had made up his mind to uphold her in everything, it was far better not to raise any discussion.

" Now I like a woman who has the sense to take a man at his word. I told her she was to get everything she wanted for herself and the child, and to have the bills sent to me. There are plenty of women who would have been shy about ordering things, but I am glad Amy is not one of them."

" She does not seem very shy, I must say," remarked Letty. " And I hope she is not very extravagant."

"Extravagant!" cried Sir John. "I should say certainly not. Of course, as my son's widow, and the mother of my heir, she is entitled to have everything she wants, and everything of the very best. She is entitled,

I say, and I beg, Letty, that neither you nor
your aunt will throw out the slightest hint
about extravagance! She must not be made
uncomfortable just as she comes to us, poor
girl. I am going to get the family diamonds
out for her. They have been at Coutts' ever
since your poor dear mother died, Letty.
My poor boy always said, 'Keep them for
her until she comes home.' He would not
let me send them to India."

"She cannot wear them while she is in
deep mourning," said Letty.

"Never mind, she can have them to play
with and to look at. And they are worth
looking at, too. They were given to a Lady
Erskine in the time of Charles the First as a
wedding present, and the necklace alone is
worth over a hundred thousand pounds."

"I think you had better keep them yourself, papa, when they come here. Amy may
not care for the responsibility."

"Oh! but I have got a fire and burglarproof safe put up in her bedroom," said Sir John, "in which they will be perfectly safe. I mean to give her one key and keep the other myself. And now I must send off a telegram to tell her to expect us soon after three this afternoon, and she had better engage a couple of rooms for us for a night or two; we must stay with her until she has all her shopping done."

"I think I had better stay here to receive you all," said Aunt Louise. "You will not want me in town."

So it was arranged, and a telegram was despatched to announce the arrival of Sir John and Letty that same afternoon.

"I begin to feel quite nervous!" said Letty, as she and her father were on their way to the Grand Hotel from Victoria. "I wonder if I shall like her?"

"Of course you will like her. Why not?" said Sir John. "Your poor brother's widow?"

When the waiter threw open the door of
Mrs. John's sitting-room and announced "Sir
John Erskine and Mrs. Herbert Otway," a
young lady rose slowly from the couch on
which she was reclining, and came to meet
them. She wore a perfectly-fitting gown of
some soft material that fell in long, straight
folds from the waist and showed her beautiful full figure to the best advantage; her
abundant soft and very fair, it might almost
be called flaxen hair, lay in fluffy curls on her
forehead, and made her dark, bright and very
beautiful eyes look even darker than they
were. On her head was the daintiest and
most becoming little apology for a widow's
cap; the ruffles at her throat and wrists were
black, and they made her beautiful, pure complexion seem almost dazzling by the contrast.

A pair of small, black earrings, and a
rosary of black beads, with a large cross
attached, were her only ornaments, unless a
pince-nez, which was singularly becoming to

the form of her very beautiful face, could be considered one.

" At last, dearest Sir John !" she said, as the old man folded her in his arms and kissed her warmly. "How I have longed for this moment ! I feel now that my many troubles are over for evermore !"

That night Letty wrote to her aunt— " Amy is a little taller and very much stouter than I expected. She is very handsome, and she walks in a stately manner that is most imposing. Papa raves about her, of course, and I feel very insignificant, I assure you !"

CHAPTER XXV.

MRS. JOHN ERSKINE COMES HOME.

A week had gone by before Mrs. John Erskine announced that she was ready to leave London ; but if Letty was tired of dancing attendance upon her, not so Sir John. From the moment of their meeting he was her most devoted admirer ; and to his regard for her as the widow of his only son was added the most enthusiastic admiration for her beauty and her graceful appearance. The fascination was completed when, with her boy in her arms, she knelt before him as though to ask his blessing on the child ; and even Letty, who was for some reason or other disposed to be critical, could not deny that the graceful mother and sturdy little fellow

who clung to her, and hid his face upon her
shoulder—he was too shy to look at the
strangers—made a very pretty picture.   His
hair was of flaxen fairness like hers, but
his eyes were almost black, and Sir John
declared he was the first black-eyed Erskine
he had ever seen.   " Our eyes are always
either blue or brown," he said.

" But he is very like his dear father!   Do
you not think so ?" Mrs. John said.   " Letty,
you see the likeness, I am sure.   Darling
Jack always said baby had the Erskine nose."

" I think it must be the Gordon nose,"
Letty answered, "for he is much more like
you than poor Jack."

" Does him hear what his Auntie Letty
says ?" the picturesque young mother cried,
as she danced the child in her arms.   " She
says you are like your own mummy!   Oh!
my angel, you do not care who you are like,
do you, now you have got home to your dear
grandpapa ?"   Then, as the little fellow made

a clutch at her cap and pulled it off, she added, " Is it not strange? He always does that. I hope, dearest Sir John," and she suddenly set the child on his feet and knelt again by the old man's side, " I hope you do not think I ought to go on wearing my cap? I put it on to-day that you might not be shocked, but I never wore it at Sorrento."

" My dearest Amy, you must do exactly as you like," and Sir John put his arm round her, and drew her to him fondly. " And I really do not know whether I admire you more with it or without it."

The lovely dark eyes, that were neither blue nor black, but something between the two, which were fixed upon his face, grew soft with emotion. " Oh, Sir John," she said, and her lips quivered, " I have not heard such sweet words as those since I lost my darling." She flung herself on the old man's breast and hid her face. " And to think that I have come home to you without him," she sobbed.

As soon as she had recovered composure, Letty, who had taken little Jacky upon her lap, glanced at her curiously. She looked even handsomer than she had done before her little outburst of sorrow; there was a slight flush on her cheeks, and her pretty hair was a little ruffled; but the flow of tears, if they had flowed, had not reddened either her eyes or her nose, and Letty was angry with herself for the suspicion that the display of emotion was less genuine than it seemed.

But Sir John's captivation was complete, and the first moment he was alone with his daughter, his admiration broke into words. He had expected to see a pretty woman, but she was dignified and graceful as well; indeed, he had rarely, he might say never, seen a woman who walked so gracefully across a room as Amy did, and her appearance in the street was really most striking. He was not at all surprised to see the way men turned about to look at her. Certainly his poor, dear boy, had shown great discrimination, both as regarded appearance and manner, when he chose Amy for his wife.

The week she spent in town was not an agreeable one to Letty. Her father was entirely taken up with Mrs. John, and, whether by accident or design, Mrs. John made a point of never consulting her sister-in-law in any way. She made her plans; told Sir John what she wanted to do; he always agreed without comment or objection, and nothing was left for Letty but just to make a third in the carriage, and to sit in it patiently for hours, while Sir John, always with his cheque-book in his pocket, attended upon his handsome daughter-in-law, going with her hither and thither and paying her bills without a murmur. It is quite certain that by the time she graciously announced that she had done all her business, he was the poorer by at least three hundred pounds;

and over and above that sum, there was the by no means moderate hotel bill.

But he was one of the most generous of men, and he paid everything without a murmur ; and although he was devoted to Amy, he found time to pay sundry visits to his lawyers which resulted in an addition of £500 per annum to the £1,000 which was already settled by post-nuptial settlement upon his son's widow.   But when telling her what he had done for her, Sir John was sensible enough to inform her also that, as she would now make her home with him at the Chase, all her personal expenses and those of the child, were to be provided for out of her very ample jointure.   In reply she bestowed upon him one of her emotional caresses ; assured him that he was the dearest and most thoughtful of men, and that she had no doubt she could make fifteen hundred a year suffice for herself and little Jacky for the present.

She was an inveterate talker; but to
Letty always be it remembered, the only
critic before whom she had as yet appeared,
it seemed that in the stream of words there
was but little worthy of note. When she
talked about her winter abroad she had
nothing to say of the places she had visited
or the people she had met; everything turned
on herself; the impression she had made,
not the impression she received.

It was the same thing in London. The
shops she praised and patronised were those
in which her orders were received with what
she considered becoming deference, and if the
waiters and chambermaids at the hotel did
not fly to execute her orders she would
threaten to complain to the manager. One
afternoon Letty was not in the sitting-room
with her bonnet on when the carriage was
announced, so Mrs. John carried off her
father-in-law, and would not wait even five
minutes. Letty, rather relieved than vexed

to escape the dull round of shopping, chartered a hansom, and went off alone to spend the afternoon with some friends of her own, a proceeding with which Mrs. John professed to be much scandalised ; and she even began a little lecture on the subject, but Letty cut it short with perfect good humour.

"As long as papa sees no harm in what I did, Amy," she said, " I do not think you need trouble yourself." But from that moment the glove, as it were, was thrown down, and Letty knew that any real affection between her and her sister - in - law was impossible.

And now at last the big new travelling boxes are packed ; Sir John has signed the last cheque ; the smart servant who is to act as maid to Mrs. John, and nurse to little Jacky, is engaged, and Mrs. John herself, dressed in the smartest and most effective travelling-cloak that could by any possibility be designed for a young widow, and on her head a neat untrimmed black felt hat, leans back, looking remarkably handsome and placid, in the first - class carriage that is bearing her to her future home.

Opposite to her is Sir John, proud as a peacock, and full of admiration for the lovely young woman who does so much credit to his dead son's taste ; and in the corner at the other end of the carriage is Letty, who is trying to persuade herself that this fascinating sister-in-law is not taking more than a fair share of Sir John's love and attention, and that she is not just a little neglected. And feeling also that a somewhat changed life may be in store for her in her old home, she wishes that, without the sacrifice of her pride, she could make some overture to her husband.

"I am not at all unhappy," she said to herself, as London, where *he* lived was left farther and farther behind, "but I wish, oh, how I wish——"

"Here we are," cried Sir John. "Now,

Amy, my love, let me collect your things. Where is the dressing-bag and your writing-case? Letty, just pull that 'hold all' out of the netting over your head like a good girl. That's right. Now then." He bounced out on the platform and gave his hand to Amy, and then to the nurse who had the child in her arms. Letty stepped out by herself; delivered the "hold all," which contained Amy's wraps and umbrellas, to a porter, and then walked after Sir John, who was stepping along radiant and happy, and looking an inch taller than usual, with his beautiful daughter-in-law upon his arm.

The open barouche with the dappled greys was in readiness, and Sir John's private omnibus stood at a little distance waiting for the luggage. Mrs. John stepped into the carriage; motioned to the maid to follow with the child, and placed them beside herself on the front seat. Sir John and Letty sat with their backs to the horses.

And in that order they dashed through the High Street of Little Centre Bridge. They were seen by the Rector as he was turning in at his own gate, and by several leading ladies of the town who happened to be in Crump's shop ; they all ran to the door the moment Mrs. Sumner, who was acting as scout, said, " Here they are !" And Mrs. John, leaning back in the carriage ; saw them all, and smiled, being quite satisfied that she must make a good impression on those gaping strangers ! Sir John sat bolt upright ; very much excited, and very proud of the pretty woman with the soft fair hair and the lovely dark eyes.

" I wonder what they think of her ?" he said to himself, as he waved his hand to the Rector, and took off his hat to the ladies.

The carriage turned in at the big gates, and bowled up the drive at a smart pace ; Miss Lambton saw it coming and shed a few tender tears at the thought of the young husband in his far-away grave, even as she prepared to meet the widow with a smile; and before half-an-hour had gone by, it was known throughout the length and breadth of the town that Mrs. John Erskine had come home at last.

CHAPTER XXVI.

MRS. JOHN GETS INTO RAPTURES.

THE day of Mrs. John Erskine's long looked for arrival was not very agreeably spent by the inmates of the Chase, and yet it was impossible for anyone, except a most captious critic, to find fault with her. Miss Lambton and Letty could not be captious critics, and even when they were alone together they carefully avoided comparing notes about her ; indeed, so marked was the avoidance of the subject that it could not be put down to accident.

And it was not that there was any want of sweetness and graciousness, and an apparent desire to be well pleased with everything, in the new comer ; but with the sweetness and graciousness and the desire to be pleased, there was "a something"—that was how Letty put it to herself; while Miss Lambton, who was never very severe upon anyone, mentally compared her nephew's beautiful widow to a cat with her paws sheathed. Sir John, who saw no flaws in his new toy, took her himself, in the pride of his heart, to see the rooms he had prepared for her, as well as the nurseries for his grandson ; Miss Lambton and Letty went also, and formed, as it were, the tail of the little procession.

Mrs. John fell at once into raptures. "It was so kind of you, dearest Sir John, to take so much trouble ; everything is charming. I am delighted with it all ; but if I had only known that you were going to give me such a dear little suite all to myself—it *is* so nice to have it—I think I should have said, 'Do not furnish until I come,' as then I could have had a voice—only a *voice*, you know ; my darling husband always allowed me to

have a voice — in the arrangement. For
instance, I had set my heart upon a dado,
and they have not put one. I had a *sweet*
dado at Sorrento! Really I got quite attached
to it. Of course, this paper is *quite* lovely,
and it doesn't matter about the dado; not in
the very least; but as it was being done in
the new, you know——ah, yes! those pretty
Indian things! As you say, they are very
handsome and rich-looking, and I would not
be without them for the world, but every day
at Sorrento I used to say, 'What a treat not
to see anything Indian.' You can understand that one gets just a little tired of them
—can't you, Sir John?"

"Just what I said when papa ordered
them," whispered Letty to her aunt.

"My dear child," said Sir John, "you
must turn them all out, and get something
you like better. I want to make you feel at
home, don't you see? You must say what
you would like instead of all these rugs and

things, and there is no reason why we should not have a dado."

"Oh, dear no!   Pray do not think of it. A dado with that paper would never do!   I must be satisfied, and I really don't mind about the Indian things; only, you can fancy that, just at present, they bring back past happy days too vividly.   But I shall get used to them, and to——everything.   The room is really *very* pretty ; a shade heavy-looking perhaps, but that may be only because every-thing was so light and bright at Sorrento. And this is my bedroom.   Very pretty! *very* pretty indeed.   I am charmed.   But why, dearest Sir John, did you not just write and say, 'Amy, which do you like best, pink or blue?'   I have quite a morbid and ridiculous dislike to pink.   I think I must ask to have everything blue."

"Of course, my dear girl.   Of course ; anything you like.   I wish I had thought of asking you ; but someone said — Letty, I think — that you would be sure to like pink."

"It was very sweet of her to decide for me," and Mrs. John gave Letty a smile. "And nothing can be prettier than pink. Everything was blue at Sorrento. The sky and the sea, and my bedroom furniture. Quite *en suite*, as that horrid creature, Rossitur, used to say. She was very proud of the little bits of French and Italian she had picked up. And now for the nurseries. I am rather sorry they open out of my room, do you know ; but, of course, I can lock myself in. I had the nurseries at Sorrento as far away from my bedroom as possible. Morning sleep is essential to me, and I am afraid I must ask for a double door here to shut out Master Jacky's noise. I always had a delicious morning sleep at Sorrento. A double door will not be very troublesome, will it, dear Sir John ?"

"Troublesome ! Not at all ! And what if

it were ?   You must have what you like.
This is the night nursery," opening a door.
"Any improvement you can suggest here ?"

"No, this seems all right.   There is only
one thing that I must mention.   My precious
child must have his head to the north, and
with the cot that way it will be to the south.
And I am afraid I must ask you to have my
bed turned too ; I like to feel that I have
got the magnetic current all right.   I always
slept with my head to the north at Sorrento ;
and it makes the greatest difference in my
dreams.   You have all got your heads to the
north, I hope ?"

"I never know whether I am north, south,
east, or west," cried Sir John.   "But you
must have what you like, my dear."

They were back in Mrs. John's bedroom
by that time.   "Let's see—which is the
north ?" he added, turning round and round.
"I'm hanged if I know."

With some difficulty the north was found ;

but the desired aspect proved a very incon-
venient position for the bed, and it was
finally arranged that it should stand in the
middle of the room according to the Indian
fashion.

" How I shall miss my cosy little nest at
Sorrento," was the last thing Letty heard as
they all went down stairs again.

Aunt Louise had taken great pains in the
ordering of Mrs. John's first dinner at the
Chase, and the cook had taken great pains
in the dressing of it; but, somehow, it failed
to hit the lady's fancy. She could not touch
thin soup, and " salmon cutlets always made
her ill;" but although she had some objection
to make to every dish, she contrived to make
a very hearty meal.

In the drawing - room afterwards she
stretched herself on a couch, saying that
she always lay down for half-an-hour after
dinner at Sorrento; but she did not go to
sleep as Miss Lambton fondly hoped she

would do ; she talked incessantly, and the
first subject she started was the estrangement between Herbert Otway and Letty.

" I really must try what I can do," she
said.   " Has anyone tried *seriously* to bring
you together ?"

" I do not wish to discuss the matter, Amy,
if you please," Letty rejoined.   " No one
talks of it here, and I do not see why you
should begin."

" But I mean to take it up very seriously,
and as a matter of duty," said Mrs. John.
" I am quite sure it only requires a little
judicious management ; and that it is not
likely to get from anyone but myself.   I do
hope he will not take it into his head to fall
in love with *me*.   It would be very awkward,
and I have the oddest fancy that he will, you
know.   There was such a funny little man at
Sorrento who was quite wild about me.   He
used to leave flowers at the villa.   Was it
not romantic ?   I am not sure that he did not

go to Vico and drown himself. A man did commit suicide there one day."

"We must not let anything so dreadful happen to Mr. Otway," said Letty, composedly; but she felt far from tranquil inwardly. "Rather than run such a risk for him, I should be tempted to come to the rescue myself!"

"Oh! can anyone tell me if Walter Duncombe has come to the Hermitage?" Mrs. John changed the subject quickly. "You know he was in Jack's regiment. He got the property, we heard, on the death of his uncle; but have you seen anything of him?"

"We have not seen him," Letty answered. "I know papa called when he came home, and he left a card, but he has been away all the winter."

"He is expected home this week," said Miss Lambton. "So Dr. Murray told me yesterday."

"I must ask dear Sir John to call again;

not that he was a very intimate friend—I had many more intimate in India—but still, it would be pleasant to see one of the regiment again."

"Jack did not like him, I think, did he?" asked Letty.

"Well, he did, and he didn't," Mrs. John answered. "He did not like the way he made love to Rossitur; but I cannot help thinking that, if my poor darling had not interfered, Walter Duncombe would have married her. She got herself talked about a little, and her marriage with Pottinger was all but broken off; then Jack said he would not have any playing of fast and loose, and made her marry. I do not think she ever forgave him, for of course, she wanted to marry the gentleman. I wonder what has become of her? I cannot help thinking that she must have seen Walter Duncombe, or heard of him, in Italy, and that she will turn up in this neighbourhood before long. I always said he was fond of her, and she used to get great influence over people."

" Have you a photograph of her?" Letty asked.

" No; but she is really not at all unlike me," and Mrs. John laughed affectedly. " It used to make poor dear Jack so savage when anyone said it ; but if you dressed her up in my clothes you would take her for me. Horrid creature! I have lost all interest in her, she treated me so badly ; but I should like to know where she is. You mentioned someone called Murray just now, Aunt Louise. Is he your family doctor?"

" Oh, no! He is our Rector. A Doctor of Divinity, and one of our greatest friends. Mrs. Murray is sure to be here to-morrow to call upon you. Has Letty told you about the child she found and brought home?"

" That Mrs. Murray found? What an odd thing to find a child. What sort of child?"

" A dear little boy of about two years

old.   His mother deserted him at Victoria
Station, and —— what is the matter, dear?
Are you not comfortable?"

"Quite, thanks, auntie dear.   Only there
is a dreadful pin pricking me, and it made
me start.   Go on, please.   He was found at
Victoria Station by Mrs. Murray, did you
say?"

"Yes; she found him in the waiting-room,
and they were going to send the poor little
mite to the workhouse, when Mary, that is
Mrs. Murray, said she would take him home;
and so she did."

"And the mother has never come forward
to claim him," Letty added.

"And Mrs. Murray has got him now?
How very good of her to take in a stray
child.   Letty, my love, I must ask you to
look for this wretched pin.   It has put me
into a fever.   I am afraid my new maid is
not very expert."

Letty began to search among Mrs. John's

frills and laces, and presently found the offending pin.

" Thanks so much, dear." She lay silent and still for about five minutes after that ; then she suddenly raised herself to a sitting posture, and said, as she arranged the curls on her forehead, " Do you know, I cannot help thinking that the unnatural mother was Rossitur?" she said, "and that your friend has brought home little Georgy Pottinger!"

" But you will recognise him," cried Letty and her aunt in a breath.

"Oh, dear no ; I scarcely ever saw the child—not even at Sorrento," answered Mrs. John, as she threw herself back on the couch again.

END OF SECOND VOLUME.

TILLOTSON AND SON, PRINTERS, BOLTON.

www.ingramcontent.com/pod-product-compliance
Lightning Source LLC
Chambersburg PA
CBHW060520030726
47498CB00004B/1020